NORTHERN SUNSET

Ever since her brother had been mentally crippled by an accident on an oil-rig, Catriona had hated oilmen and all their doings. So she wasn't exactly ready to co-operate with Brett Simons when he arrived on her peaceful Shetland island home with grandiose plans to ruin it by setting up an oil terminal there. In the ensuing battle, could she possibly win?

AN UNBROKEN MARRIAGE

Despite what Simon Herries thought, India was *not* seriously involved with Melford Taylor, let alone callously stealing him from his wife – but Simon resolutely chose to think the worst of her. And he certainly picked a very drastic way of sorting the situation out!

ISLAND OF THE DAWN

Chloe's estranged husband Leon Stephanides might have tricked her into meeting him again in Greece and keeping her virtually a prisoner on a tiny island – but he needn't think there was going to be any reconciliation! Not when she knew all he wanted her for was to act as a smoke-screen to his relationship with Marisa!

DAUGHTER OF HASSAN

Much as she loved and respected her Arab step-father, and wanted to please him, Danielle was horrified when she realised he was planning to marry her off, in the approved Arab fashion, to his nephew Jourdan whom she hadn't even met. And if she wondered if things might just improve when she *did* meet him, she was wrong. For Jourdan was about as attractive as a snake – and twice as dangerous!

THE CAGED TIGER

Any feeling that had existed between Davina and Ruy de Silvadores, her husband and the father of her son, had long since turned to ashes – and it was only for her child's sake that Davina was now going back to Spain, to her husband and his aristocratic family. She was ready for a difficult time – but she had not anticipated the situation that awaited her . . .

NORTHERN SUNSET

BY
PENNY JORDAN

MILLS & BOON LIMITED
15-16 BROOK'S MEWS
LONDON W1A 1DR

First published 1982
Australian copyright 1982
Philippine copyright 1982
This edition 1982

© Penny Jordan 1982

ISBN 0 263 73981 3

Set in Monophoto Baskerville 11 on 11½ pt.
01–1182

Made and printed in Great Britain by
Richard Clay (The Chaucer Press) Ltd,
Bungay, Suffolk

CHAPTER ONE

MAGNUS had been right, Catriona reflected, staring helplessly at the mist which crept insidiously across the harbour as she watched. He had warned her this morning, with older-brother concern, that sea-fog had been forecast and that she would be wiser not to leave Falla, but they were low on stores and Christmas wasn't very far away. The old days when the laird's house on Falla rang to laughter over the Christmas season might have died with their parents; they might be as poor as the poorest of their crofters, but Catriona refused to let the season pass without at least some attempt to celebrate. Hence the trip to Lerwick.

Magnus had protested that she could never manage their dilapidated old fishing boat alone, but Catriona had laughed. She knew the waters round Falla and the other Shetland isles well enough to sail them in her sleep, even if the huge oil drilling platforms anchored far out to sea were new landmarks. Her normally generously curved lips tightened sharply. Oil—how she hated that word and all it stood for! Her eyes clouded as she thought of Magnus; her once strong and fearless brother, whom she had hero-worshipped all through her teens and who had willingly taken the place of their parents when they had been drowned in a sailing accident.

She searched the sea again. The meagre stores which were all her slender purse would stretch to were already on board. She had felt the sympathy

5

behind the kind enquiries as people asked after Magnus. There had been Petersons on Falla since the first Norse invasion of the islands, and Catriona knew that the surreptitious slipping of little extras in among her shopping sprang not from pity but from a genuine compassion. The people who lived on these islands of the far north had a deep appreciation of the hardships resulting from incapacity of the breadwinner of the family. The seas round the Shetlands were rich in fish, but the waters were treacherous and the winds which continually blew over them resulted in fierce storms.

There was scarcely a family on the Shetlands who did not have some grim story to relate of lives lost and limbs maimed.

It was no use, Catriona acknowledged, she was not going to be able to leave Lerwick tonight. Making sure that the yaol was properly secured, she headed away from the harbour, a small, finely built girl, with silver-blonde hair curling on to her shoulders, an inheritance from those far distant Norse ancestors who had claimed these windswept islands as their own. The inhabitants of the Shetlands might no longer speak the ancient Norn tongue, but in tradition and outlook they were closer to their Scandinavian cousins than their dour Scots neighbours.

Only Catriona's eyes showed the Celtic blood of her mother, the soft-spoken redhead her father had met in Edinburgh during his university days and married; they were grey, the colour of the seas round Falla, changing with the light from softest grey to deep violet. More than one male had been captivated by Catriona's delicately moulded beauty during her brief years in London training as a librarian, but when Magnus had had his accident she had ruthlessly cut herself off from that life and returned to their childhood home to be with the brother who needed her so badly.

She paused to stare blindly into a brightly decorated shop window, her eyes misting with tears. It was all very well for Mac to assure her that there was nothing physically wrong with Magnus and that it was a mercy that he had not been killed or seriously injured, but the man who now sat staring into space in the huge, dilapidated house on Falla was not the brother Catriona remembered from her youth, alive and alert, teasing, driving her mad with his older-brother superiority and then flying home from Oman that terrible night when they brought the news that their parents had been drowned off Bressay.

She would never forget his care and understanding then; he had been her rock in the storm of grief which had swept her, his concern total and healing, and now that it was her turn to be his rock she would not desert him.

Mac had warned her that it might be years, if ever, before Magnus recovered. He had brought them both into the world, and Catriona knew he shared her helpless grief for Magnus. They had all been so proud of him when he went to Oxford ... There was no point in dwelling on the past, Catriona reminded herself. After his accident Magnus had been offered an office job by his company, but he had refused it, retreating to Falla where he could shut out the rest of the world and forget.

A night in Lerwick was an expense she would rather have avoided, Catriona reflected. Without Magnus's salary their only source of income was a small pension. Even if she were qualified there was no employment on Falla for a librarian; the crofters fished their living from the sea, and Catriona had learned to close her eyes to the deterioration of their once luxurious home.

She paused outside the hotel she had used on happier occasions—those infrequent visits home from London when Magnus had managed to get leave to coincide with hers. He had been very generous in those days, giving her an allowance as well as paying for her education. Although only seven years separated them he had willingly shouldered the responsibility of providing for her after their parents' death. Carefully checking the money in her purse, Catriona went inside. Like most of the hotels in Lerwick, it was run as a family concern. The girl behind the reception desk remembered Catriona and greeted her with a smile.

'How's your brother?' she enquired sympathetically. 'But he was lucky, wasn't he?'

If one considered that lying paralysed on the ground while all around one the world went up in flames, filled with the screams of the dying, then yes, Magnus had been lucky, Catriona acknowledged, but the girl meant well, so she smiled and asked if they had a vacant room.

'I'm sorry, Miss Peterson, but we don't. You see, a party of oilmen flew in from Aberdeen this afternoon and can't get out again until the weather lifts.'

Oilmen! Catriona grimaced distastefully over the word. The Shetlanders had learned to live with their intrusion into their lives; to accept their busied coming and going from the mainland to the huge oil terminal at Sullom Voe and the sea-rigs.

'Look,' the receptionist suggested helpfully, 'I'll

ask them if they'll mind doubling up and leaving a room free for you. I'm sure they won't. They're out at the moment, but I'll get someone to shift their things and tell them when they come back.'

She spoke with the assurance of someone inured to climatic conditions which could suddenly imprison travellers against their will, and pored thoughtfully over the register, before pencilling out a name and writing Catriona's in its place.

She herself had no compunction about depriving the man of his room. And besides, hadn't Magnus often said that oilmen could sleep anywhere?

She hadn't bothered to bring a change of clothes, but there was a chemist's where she could buy a toothbrush and other necessities and she could rinse her undies out to dry overnight. Thanking the girl with a grateful smile, she slipped out once again into the murky afternoon.

It was dark already, but she found her way unerringly to the small chemist's. He too asked after Magnus, and Catriona supplied him with a noncommittal answer. In her handbag was the prescription Mac had given her for the sleeping tablets Magnus needed to stop him having those terrible nightmares where he relived his accident over and over again. Physically her brother was as he had always been, but mentally he was maimed and crippled, a victim of the paralysing fear inherited from his accident.

Shivering, Catriona stepped out into the street, her vivid imagination picturing the scene; the unending oilfields and tank farms; the hot desert sands; all so clearly drawn for her in Magnus's letters home. For as long as Catriona could remember he had wanted to be a geologist, and he had loved his job with United Oil. But to them he was just another employee, expendable and unimportant. Impotent anger flared in her eyes, her hatred of the huge oil conglomerates and everything they stood for overwhelming her. Magnus had once been a part of that world; the world of oil and tough, hard men, but all that had ended in the Middle East on a night of terror and pain when the black sky had turned scarlet with hungry flames and people sitting safely behind desks many thousands of miles away had been too greedy to take precautions to remove their men from the danger of Arab insurrectionists, who had swept the huge oilfield with bombs and machinegun fire, and Magnus, stunned by a vicious blow from a rifle, had had to lie helpless behind the flames until he was rescued.

The mental agony he had endured could never be atoned for, and Catriona's hatred for the men who had allowed this to happen to her brother had grown over the months of watching him fight against the fear that night had bred deep inside him.

Until it was conquered he refused to return to his work, claiming that he was useless as a geologist while he carried this terrible burden of fear and that he could not trust himself in any situation where men's lives might be at stake, not to turn and flee like a terrified child.

It was this knowledge of the extent of his fear which tormented him night and day, and which Mac and Catriona were fighting so desperately to overcome, and as her brother lost heart, Catriona's rage grew. If United Oil had been more caring of its employees and less greedy for its oil Magnus would not be hiding himself away on Falla, blenching at every mention of other oilmen, sickened by the thought that he could no longer include himself among their number. Oilmen were fearless; and it was this myth which Catriona was fighting so valiantly to explode. Everyone knew fear; and she was sure that once Magnus could be brought to accept this he would be well on the way to recovery.

Mac had said that Magnus might recover faster among other people, but her brother flatly refused to leave Falla, sinking into the withdrawn silences which so dismayed Catriona as she remembered how he used to be. What he was suffering from was something akin to shell-shock, or so Mac had told her. Catriona only knew that she would give anything to have her brother restored to his old self. He had not even demurred when Catriona told him that she was giving up her training course in order to be with him—a sure sign that he was not his normal self.

The small hotel foyer was crowded when Catriona got back. A group of men stood by the bar, their presence filling the room; tall, rugged and dressed in worn denims and tough leather jackets, they proclaimed their trade to Catriona without her needing to overhear a word of their conversation. Oilmen! She turned her back on them with bitter eyes. She hated them and everything they stood for. That her hatred was illogical she could not deny, but that did not make it any the less real, and she acknowledged that its existence was due to Magnus's accident.

One of them, a tall burly redhead, caught her eye as she squeezed past on her way to the reception desk. She gave him a freezing look in response to his openly admiring smile and as she turned her head, saw him address a comment to the man standing beside him facing the bar. The man turned, green eyes raking Catriona assessingly, a helmet pushed back on thick dark hair, his appearance that of a man accustomed to giving rather than receiving orders. Something in his glance made Catriona's anger quicken; it was not appreciative as his red-headed companion's had been, but rather dismissive, and Catriona felt herself flushing beneath his cool appraisal. The redhead spoke and his eyebrows rose, and Catriona knew beyond doubt that she was the subject of their conversation. His eyes dwelt for a moment on the soft thrust of her breasts beneath the thick Shetland wool jumper she was wearing and were then averted as he made some response.

What had they been saying about her? Catriona wondered as she reached the reception desk. Since her return to the island she had had nothing to do with the oilmen, but she had heard surprisingly good reports of them from the crofters and knew that several of the local girls had found themselves boy-friends from their ranks. There had been no tentative, shy admiration in the look she had received, though. It had been openly and blatantly sardonic. Long after the man ought to have been forgotten and her dinner had been consumed, Catriona found him lingering intrusively in her thoughts. The noise from the bar was steadily growing in volume; signs that the oilmen were enjoying themselves and obviously intended to continue doing so, and rather than return to the bar Catriona decided to go straight to her room.

The owner of the hotel was behind the reception desk and greeted her like an old friend. She asked for her key and checked the weather forecast for the morning. As she had hoped, it was good.

'You'll get nothing like this on Falla?' Richard

Nicholson murmured, glancing towards the bar.

'No, thank goodness!'

The asperity in Catriona's voice made him frown.

'They're no a bad bunch really. Noisy perhaps, but it's natural that they should want to let off steam after a turn on the rigs. You'll have been stocking up for Christmas,' he commented when Catriona made no response. 'How is Magnus?'

'Getting better,' Catriona replied noncommittally.

'Well, I'd best be on my way to bed. I've got an early start in the morning.'

They chatted for a few more minutes before Catriona managed to escape when the telephone rang. Her bedroom was a double with one huge bed, some old-fashioned furniture and a washbasin in one corner. She mentally reviewed the long trek to the bathroom and the danger of lurking oilmen and decided to make do with a thorough wash. It was too early to go to bed and she regretted the large package of paperbacks stowed on the boat. She had a newspaper in her handbag and she unearthed it, reading all the local news with a sense of nostalgia. When she was a child a visit to Lerwick had been a much looked forward to treat. Her parents had been comfortable rather than wealthy, but following their death the shares from which her father had received his main income had dropped in value, and it had been just as well that Magnus had been working. They did, of course, receive small rents from the crofters who farmed Falla, but these were tiny; a mere drop in the ocean when compared with the costs of running the Great House.

The noise from downstairs seemed to increase rather than diminish. Locking the door and placing the key on the dressing table, Catriona stripped off and rinsed her undies out before placing them by the hot radiator.

Fortunately the bedroom was pleasantly warm, but by the time she was ready for bed she was beginning to shiver. She could hardly sleep in her jeans and jumper, she decided ruefully, eyeing her damp underclothes as she slid beneath the cotton sheets, and yet she felt decidedly vulnerable lying beneath the covers with nothing on.

Her last thought as sleep claimed her was of her journey home and her sincere hopes that the weather would lift. She could not afford to spend another night in Lerwick.

She awoke with a start, staring round the room for the origins of the sound which had disturbed her sleep, and then froze as she found it; all six foot odd of it, leaning against the closed bedroom door.

'Well, well, what a surprise,' a deep male voice drawled mockingly. 'But I think you've got the wrong room. Alex is down the hall.'

He moved quickly—so quickly that Catriona barely had time to grasp the bedclothes protectively around her as he bent to yank them back.

'What do you think you're doing?' she gasped furiously, only too aware of his intention as he loomed over her, his fingers tightening on the covers. Her heart jolted painfully as her eyes grew accustomed to the darkness and she saw the unmistakable features of the dark-haired man from the bar, minus his helmet but still wearing his air of casual arrogance.

'I'm the one who should be asking you that,' he replied imperturbably. 'How did you get in here, and just what the hell do you think you're doing? If I want a woman I'm perfectly capable of finding myself one.'

Dark colour surged over Catriona's pale skin as she realised the import of what he was saying. He thought she was actually waiting for him!

'Like I said,' he drawled in hard tones, 'Alex is sleeping down the hall. I'll give you two minutes to get out of my bed and into his, otherwise I call the manager.'

Catriona's mind whirled, her first stammered words wildly different from the cold snub she had intended to deliver, as she stammered anxiously:

'I can't . . . I'm not dressed . . .'

The look in his eyes made her bite her lip in mortification. Of all the stupid things to say—but there was something about lying here completely naked beneath these sheets, with this sardonic brute of a man standing over her hurling all manner of unwarranted accusations at her, that made her feel decidedly at a disadvantage. What she ought to have done, she decided, simmering with anger, was to call his bluff and demand that he did call the manager. His room indeed! And where had he got the key?

That was answered with his next words.

'I suppose I ought to have been prepared for something like this when they couldn't find my key and had to use the pass-key, but like I said, little lady, I do my own hunting. Now get dressed and get out of here!'

He stood back from the bed, arms folded over a broad chest which tapered to lean hips and long, well muscled legs, his stance plainly that of a man determined to have his own way.

'You get out!' Catriona demanded breathlessly, suddenly finding her voice, and ignoring the warning look in his eyes with a reckless disregard for danger. 'This is my room,' she told him firmly, ignoring the sardonic expression with which he was studying her. 'If you don't believe me, go down and ask at reception. They were fully booked and said that they were going to ask someone to double up.'

'Very plausible,' he scoffed. 'How do I know that I can believe you? For all I know you could be some cheap little tart intent on making some easy money.'

Catriona gasped and would have shot upright in protest, if she hadn't remembered just in time how badly she needed the protection of the bedclothes.

'How dare you!' she seethed. 'You come in here, making vile accusations, demanding that I leave, threatening to call the manager. If anyone's going to call him, it will be me—to have you thrown out!'

'Be my guest,' her persecutor goaded, holding open the door. Catriona glanced wildly from the empty passage to her damp underclothes, well out of reach, and then glared angrily across the room.

'Go away and let me get dressed and then I will.'

'And let you escape scot free to go and play your tricks on someone else?' He shook his head sardonically. 'I've told you already, you should have picked Alex. He would have been far more amenable.'

Catriona took a deep, steadying breath. Alex presumably was the burly redhead. 'And I've told you,' she announced through gritted teeth, 'you've got it all wrong. This is my room. You're the intruder.'

Tears weren't far away, and the green eyes narrowed suddenly, his expression changing. 'Convince me. If you're not just a local girl out for a good time, who are you? And what are you doing here?'

'My name is Catriona Peterson. If you don't believe me ask the owner of the hotel,' Catriona told him, enraged at being forced to undergo this inquisition. 'And if it hadn't been for this sea-mist I'd have been on my way back to Falla by now.'

'Falla?' The sharp enquiry startled her. 'You live there?'

When Catriona nodded his expression seemed to change, but he made no further mention of the island, saying dryly instead, 'Well, Catriona Peterson, always supposing you're telling me the truth, how do you suggest we resolve our present dilemma, which is, as I see it, that the two of us are both laying claim to this one bed?'

No apology for his earlier insults, Catriona seethed inwardly. Typical of his breed, though, the big tough guy who could never admit to being wrong.

'No dilemma,' she assured him curtly. 'I suggest you go downstairs and check with reception and they'll tell you who you're sharing with.'

It was plain that he wasn't used to being given orders. His eyes gleamed in the dark, and their expression made Catriona shrink back against the bed.

'Oh no,' he said softly. 'This is my room, booked in my name, and I don't intend giving it up to share a bed with Alex.' He moved towards the door as he spoke, closing it firmly and turning the key before coming across to the bed and stripping off his leather jacket.

Appalled, Catriona stared disbelievingly at him.

'You're not . . . You're not sleeping here!' she managed to get out at last, furious with herself for making the words seem more of a question than a statement.

'Why not?' came the cool response. 'After all, it is my room, and if I'm going to have to share with one of you, I think I prefer you to Alex. You could, of course, always leave,' he taunted. His fingers were on the buttons of the checked plaid shirt he was wearing, and Catriona stared desperately at the door, bitterly regretting her fastidious refusal to sleep in her underwear. In that at least she would have been able to leave the bed and grab her clothes. Even sleeping downstairs in a chair would be preferable to sharing a bed with this man!

'What's the matter?' he jeered as she remained immobile.

She wasn't going to ask him to leave so that she could get dressed—he would probably refuse anyway and take delight in humiliating her by doing so. Her face burned as she dwelt on having to endure him watching her dress.

'If you had the slightest scrap of decency you would leave this room right now,' she announced in freezing accents, trying to read his reaction to her words.

It shocked her with its comprehensive grasp of her feelings. 'But then men like me don't have, do they?' he demanded softly. 'At least not in your eyes. What is it with you?'

Catriona moved slightly, the moonlight briefly touching her hair, turning it silver. His eyes followed the movement, widening slightly.

'So it's you . . .' he drawled in recognition. 'I saw you in the bar. . . .'

'And I saw you,' Catriona whipped back. 'And you're quite right, I don't like men like you. I detest them, and everything they stand for.' Her lip curled faintly as she forgot her fear. 'You're quite safe with me—I wouldn't touch you for all the oil in the North Sea!'

He was pulling off his shirt, and his hands stilled,

his eyes like jade as they held hers, compelling them to witness the undeniable maleness of his hair toughened chest as the shirt was discarded.

'Is that a fact?'

'I can't stay here with you,' Catriona protested, forgetting her earlier determination not to plead with him. 'Just let me get dressed and . . .'

'And get the manager, who'll turf me out of my room, and no doubt accuse me of seducing you into the bargain. No way,' he told her curtly. 'You're staying right there. Unless of course you're brave enough to get out of that bed and get the key?'

He knew she couldn't, Catriona admitted wrathfully as he turned his back on her and calmly turned on the basin tap. If only he had been going to have a bath, she could have left while he was gone. The suspicion that he was deliberately punishing her by remaining would not be denied. He could have as little desire to share the bed with her as she did with him, but he had sensed her fear beneath her anger, and meant to punish her by arousing it still further. Her shocked ears caught the unmistakable sound of more clothes being removed, and the wardrobe she had left untouched was opened and a case dragged out.

'Seems to me whoever was supposed to tell me that you had my room also forgot to get my luggage removed,' he drawled coolly from the other side of the bed. 'Unless you were lying all along?'

'No. . . .'

This time she made no attempt to conceal her panic, rolling as close to the edge of the bed as she could as she felt it depress with his weight. Her heart was thudding like a sledgehammer, and she had never felt less like sleep. Her companion turned over

and she froze, unaware of the small protest she had
uttered until his fingers grasped her chin, sending
shocked fear washing over her.

'Something tells me you've never done this before,'
he murmured, in a voice which, for the first time,
held a thread of humour. 'Would I be right?'

More right than he knew, Catriona acknowledged
wryly. She hadn't slept with any man yet, never
mind one who was a complete stranger, and even
though she prided herself on being a modern girl,
his presence overwhelmed her, conscious as she was
of his unembarrassed nudity, so totally and frankly
male.

As she fought against the panic his touch had
aroused, Catriona heard him add softly,

'Too scared to reply?'

Her tense muscles gave him the answer she was
incapable of speaking, and she thought she heard
him sigh as his thumb stroked softly along her gritted
jaw bone.

'You're quite safe,' he assured her gravely. 'I'm
not about to ravish you. All I want is a decent night's
sleep. We've been out on the rigs for the last five
days, in a force nine gale, and believe me,' he told
her frankly. 'Even if I wanted to I doubt I could
summon the energy to teach you how to make love.'

'I don't need anyone to teach me!' Catriona
choked back, furious with both him and herself. By
rights they shouldn't be having this conversation.
They were complete strangers.

He laughed and she felt the sound shake his
body—a body which she was acutely conscious was
as naked as her own—and colour flamed momentarily along her cheekbones, curiosity mingling with
outrage, a strange desire to know more about this

man who treated their presence in bed together as though it were of no more moment than a casual chance meeting at a bus stop.

'Don't touch me!' she demanded, jerking away from the hand which cupped her chin, gasping with pain as hard fingers suddenly seized her wrists, pulling her against the male body she had mentally been contemplating, its weight pinning her back against the mattress as cool masculine lips feathered lightly against the full softness of her own.

Catriona knew enough about men to know there was nothing of passion in the kiss. It was firm, experienced, and totally platonic, just as the male contours of the body now dominating her own were completely and absolutely devoid of sexual intensity. Before she could protest she was released to listen in bitter chagrin to the male voice whispering in her ear.

'You see? And now that I've disposed of your girlish fears perhaps we can both get some sleep.'

There was a pause while she struggled to formulate a suitably crushing response, and then he added suavely, 'Disappointed?'

The sardonic question released her anger to spill out over him in heated denial. Disppointed? She glared at him with loathing. Never in a thousand years! How could he have inflicted such humiliation upon her? And yet at the back of her mind was an emotion, far too tenuous to be given a name, which niggled tormentingly.

'Now go to sleep,' she was instructed in much the same tones one might use to an erring child, and much to her own astonishment she found that her eyes were closing; the sleep she had denied she would ever experience washing over her in waves.

Some time during the night those same waves were transformed to the beating fury of the North Sea which had destroyed her parents' sailing dinghy and robbed them of life, and her cries of protest were drowned out by the roaring sound of the water, until as always she found sanctuary in Magnus's protective arms and the storm was spent.

When she awoke she was alone in the bed, no trace of its other occupant visible anywhere in the room, and on trembling legs Catriona sped to the door, making sure it was locked and leaving her key in the lock while she washed and dressed hurriedly, trying not to remember the events of the previous night.

How dared he think she had actually been waiting for him! She pulled her jeans on viciously, breaking a nail, and cursing as she searched for an emery board. When you lose your temper it always rebounds on you, her mother had told her when she was a child, and surveying the broken nail with a fierce frown Catriona was forced to reflect on the truth of this statement.

Just how much she had been dreading coming face to face with her unwanted room-mate Catriona could only acknowledge when she got downstairs and found the dining room empty. At least he had had the decency to make himself scarce this morning, she reflected over her breakfast, but that did not excuse him for his behaviour of the previous night. She felt the colour wash over her skin as she remembered the cool feel of his flesh against hers. She started to tremble and dismissed the thought. It was over now, and if she had any sense she would simply forget about it.

She had confined her hair in a neat plait to keep

it out of the way and she looked closer to sixteen than twenty-two as she headed for the harbour. Her body felt lethargic—a legacy from last night's nightmare. Her lips curved into a fond smile as she remembered the deep sense of protective security she had experienced as she dreamed of Magnus's comforting arms.

CHAPTER TWO

IT was a four-hour journey to Falla, but Catriona, wearing workmanlike oilskins over her jumper and jeans, worked efficiently, nursing the old fishing yaol across the windswept winter sea. The open cockpit offered scant protection from the elements, but Catriona was barely aware of the fierce wind teasing tendrils of hair which had escaped from her plait, as she concentrated of manoeuvring the unwieldy craft through the dangerous cross-currents. There was something about this battle with the wind and sea that exhilarated, setting her free from all worries and cares.

At last the sheer red sandstone cliffs of Falla came in sight and Catriona started to edge the boat into the smaller of the two deep voes which formed Falla's natural harbour. The larger voe was a true glacial fiord, Magnus had once told her, and its smooth red walls stretched endlessly down into the deep sea-water inlet.

A clutch of houses huddled together by the harbour as though seeking protection from the wind, and as Catriona moved to secure the boat the door

to one opened and gnarled fisherman came out,
smiling warmly as he hurried to help.

'Thanks, Findlay,' Catriona gasped, as he took
the rope and stretched out a hand to help her ashore.
She leapt nimbly from the deck, surefooted among
the muddle of lobster pots and coiled ropes which
littered the harbour.

'I'll help you get this stuff into the Land Rover,'
he offered, swinging up one of the large boxes with
effortless ease.

He was the same age as their father would have
been had he lived, and had taught both Peterson
children to sail and fish, and Catriona felt about him
as she did all the crofters; they were part of her
family.

It didn't take long to get the provisions loaded
into the ancient Land Rover. The village was quiet,
the men out fishing, and refusing a cup of tea,
Catriona climbed into the Land Rover and switched
on the engine.

The unmade road climbed out of the village and
across the peat moors; carpeted with wild flowers in
summer, but now in winter, grim and bleak with no
tree or bush to break the windswept turf. Here and
there were neat bare patches where the villagers had
removed peat to heat their fires. There was no coal
or wood on the islands and although these luxuries
had been imported lavishly during Catriona's
parents' time, now the fires of the Great House were
heated by the same means as those in the crofts.

The road ran past the highest part of the island,
the crumbling remains of a single tower all that was
left of the once proud castle built during the turbulent times of the wicked Earl Patrick, who had once
ruled these islands with cruelty and cunning.

The Great House was built in sandstone, overlooking a small loch, its gardens protected from the fierce wind by the sheltering hill which rose behind it. Falla had good pastures and during the summer the cows and sheep grew fat and contented. The once beautiful heather garden looked neglected and bedraggled as Catriona drove slowly through the huge wrought iron gates imported from England by the eighteenth-century Peterson who had commissioned this elegant Georgian building.

The library, which faced out on to the drive, was the room Catriona and Magnus used most. The once elegant and gracious drawing rooms were now closed off, gathering dust and falling into disrepair. At first on her return Catriona had been shocked and distressed by this, but gradually this had faded under the burden of struggling to keep even one room reasonably warm, look after her brother, manage their finances and feed them.

Magnus was standing by the window watching for her—a good sign, and she pulled up hurriedly, lifting one of the smaller boxes from the Land Rover.

Magnus opened the door for her, Russet, his red setter, jumping up enthusiastically to welcome Catriona home.

As she kissed his cheek Catriona could not help comparing her brother's gaunt features with those of the man who had invaded her bedroom.

Magnus was twenty-nine and his bulky sweater hung loosely on what had once been a well-built frame. His hair was as fair as Catriona's, his eyes a deep blue, but where laughter had once lurked in their depths there was now only pain. He never discussed the accident with her, because he wanted to protect her, she acknowledged, but when would he realise that she was no longer a little girl to be sheltered from life's blows?

He followed her down the stone-flagged hall to the kitchen, and Catriona dumped her box on the large wooden table, heaving a sigh of relief.

'Get everything you wanted?' Magnus enquired, investigating the contents curiously.

'Everything I could afford,' Catriona told him wryly. 'Lerwick has become fantastically expensive—another legacy from the oil rigs, I suppose.'

She had her back to Magnus and didn't see his faint frown at her acerbic tone. He pushed the box away and came to stand beside her, his arm round her shoulders.

'Aren't you finding it a bit heavy?' he asked her gently.

Nonplussed, Catriona stared at him. This was her usual day for baking and breadmaking and she wanted to check the old-fashioned kitchen range before she started.

'That chip you're carrying,' Magnus explained. 'Look, Cat, I appreciate your concern and loyalty, but what happened to me was an accident, pure and simple—there's no point in blaming oil for it, nor on feeding this silly hatred of everything connected with it.'

Catriona's fingers curled into her palms. She found it impossible to understand how Magnus could so calmly accept what had happened.

'Leave all that,' he said suddenly. 'Come into the library, there's something I want to show you.'

Mystified, Catriona allowed him to propel her out into the chilly hall and into the library.

A peat fire burned brightly in the immense hearth

and Catriona sank gratefully into a leather chair, her hands outstretched to the flames.

'You do too much,' Magnus told her gently. 'You shouldn't have given up your training, Cat. You can't spend the rest of your life on Falla with me.'

'I don't see why not,' she argued stubbornly. 'After all, it is half my island, so you can't order me to leave, can you?'

'Perhaps not, but it's no life for a young girl.' He caught hold of her hands, studying the broken nails and calloused skin, a look of burning anger in his eyes.

'God, Cat, I've been so selfish, but all that's going to change.'

Catriona stared at him, a joyful smile trembling on her lips. 'Magnus. . . . You can't mean you're going back to work?'

He frowned.

'No, I can't do that. Oh, I could do the routine work all right; but sooner or later I would find myself in a situation that I'm not capable of handling now. Sooner or later someone's life is going to be at risk, and I'm not going to be able to cope. That's what being a geologist is all about.'

'Strange,' Catriona murmured dryly, not wanting him to see her disappointment. 'I thought it was about looking for minerals.'

'Often in remote and dangerous parts of the world,' Magnus insisted. 'In situations where you've got to be able to rely on the other members of your team, and what sane man could trust his life to me now. . . .'

His bitterness made her want to cry.

'Oh, Magnus, you don't know that. . . .'

'Oh yes, I do,' he said with bitter finality. 'Don't

you think I've not been over and over it all these last few months? It's over, Cat. As a geologist I'm finished, but that doesn't mean the end of everything. I got this yesterday, it came after you'd left.' He handed her an envelope.

The mailboat called once a week, and Catriona stared at the impressively typed letter. It was addressed to the owners of Falla Island, and her colour faded, as she read and re-read it, her lips pursed together in an angry line.

'Magnus, we can't possibly agree to this!' she protested as she put it down. 'An oil terminal on Falla? They must be mad!'

'Not necessarily,' Magnus contradicted. There was a briskness in his voice which made Catriona glance curiously at him. On his return from hospital and during the long months which had followed he had seemed to share her bitter hatred of all things oil completely, but now she was forced to admit that she must have misjudged his sentiments.

'Come and look at this,' he commanded, opening his desk and getting out a map of the island. It was one he himself had drawn while he was at university, and although only a week ago seeing him take such an interest in things would have filled her with joy, now Catriona felt only apprehension as she watched him unroll the map and study it deeply before calling her over.

'Here's Falla Voe, and next to it the harbour. You remember how I once told you how these voes were formed during the Ice Age and how unimaginably deep they are?' When Catriona nodded he continued enthusiastically, 'You've seen how successful the oil terminal at Sullom Voe is—well, what the construction company are planning is a much smaller but similar operation here, to be used as a back-up system.'

'But it would ruin Falla,' Catriona protested, hardly able to believe her ears. Surely Magnus couldn't be in favour of it?

'Come with me.'

Taking her hand, he led her from the library and back out into the hall, throwing open the huge double doors to the drawing room. The plaster ceiling was tinged with mould, the furniture covered in dusty sheets, the whole room permeated with an unpleasant damp odour. Silently Catriona stared at her brother, wondering why he had brought her here.

'Don't you see?' he said gently. 'With the money we would get for allowing them to build the terminal this house could be restored to what it once was. We could buy a new generator instead of having to rely on one that runs on a hope and prayer. You could go back to London.' He placed his hands on her shoulders and studied her intently. 'I know how you feel about the oil industry, Cat, but you mustn't let it ruin your life—and not just yours,' he added inexorably, drawing her to the window. 'Think of our people and how much this could mean to them. They're barely scratching a living here; as soon as the children are old enough they're leaving. Do you honestly want Falla to become just another deserted island, empty of people?'

'And do you honestly want to sell your birthright for . . . for an oil terminal on your doorstep?' Catriona protested. 'It would ruin Falla, Magnus. . . .' She could hardly believe that he was actually serious. They were poor, yes, but they could manage. But could they? She remembered uneasily how quickly her slender store of money had disappeared in Lerwick; already they were dependent on the crofters for milk and vegetables from their gardens; Catriona had returned to Falla too late to make use of its brief summer, and those same crofters who generously shared their produce with them were, as Magnus had reminded her, poor themselves. Was she being selfish in wanting to keep Falla as it had always been? A fierce wave of hatred seized her. Wherever she turned it all came back to the same thing: oil. If it hadn't been for oil Magnus would be whole and well and there would be no need to even contemplate this . . . this rape of their home.

'So you're in favour?'

Her eyes begged him to deny it, and for a moment Magnus's face softened.

'I think we should at least let them do some explorative work, for the sake of the islanders if nothing else. Don't you see, Cat,' he said softly, 'we don't have the right to deny them this opportunity, and if they do go ahead it won't spoil Falla; the Government are pretty stiff about these things. Anyway, that's a long way off, these geologists they want to send out might not find the voe suitable.'

'Geologists?' Catriona said eagerly. 'Oh, Magnus, why don't you offer to do the work? I'm sure. . . .'

'No!'

The harsh word cut across her excitement, dashing all her newly sprung hopes.

'I might know in my heart that this terminal is right for Falla, but don't expect me to take any professional interest in it. I've told you, Cat, I don't have what it takes any more. Investigating that voe means that *someone* will have to dive into those waters, examine those undersea cliffs,' he told her brutally, 'relying only on a back-up team on land. Do you think anyone would trust me to be a member of that team after what happened in the Gulf?'

The anguish in his voice made her blench.

'But, Magnus, nothing did happen. You were knocked out and left for dead. . . .'

'And when I came round I was alive and all around me my colleagues, my friends were dying in agony, and I didn't do a thing to help.'

'You couldn't do anything to help,' Catriona protested, not sure whether to be glad or sorry that he was at last discussing with her the story she had only so far heard from Mac. 'You were paralysed.'

'With fear,' Magnus said with deep loathing. 'Paralysed with fear, while all around me men were on fire.'

'You weren't paralysed with fear,' Catriona protested. 'Mac explained it all to me, Magnus, the blow you received did that. . . .'

'Oh, for God's sake stop trying to make it easier for me!' Magnus demanded harshly. 'God, I wish I had died there. You can't know the hell life has been ever since.' He dropped into a chair, his head in his hands, his shoulders shaking.

'Look at me, Cat,' he commanded bitterly. 'I'm not even a man any longer. . . .' His eyes were bleak and hopeless, arousing all her protective instincts. How could he call himself a coward when he was brave enough to endure the sight of men who he claimed would only have contempt for him, on this island which was his retreat, and for the benefit of others?

Catriona was just lifting the bread tins out of the oven when she heard the helicopter overhead. Ten minutes later there was a knock on the back door, and she went to open it, shooing away the free-range chickens who kept them supplied with eggs, a genuinely pleased smile curving her lips.

'Mac!' she exclaimed, greeting their visitor. 'We weren't expecting you today.'

She stood aside to allow the grizzled Scotsman to enter the room, grinning as he sniffed the warm bread-scented atmosphere appreciatively.

'I had to go out to one of the rigs, and I got them to drop me off here instead of Lerwick.'

'Magnus will be pleased to see you.' Catriona picked up one of the tins and expertly knocked on the bottom to remove the loaf, cutting a generous crust and spreading it with butter.

'It will give you indigestion,' she warned as Mac took it from her, busying herself with the old-fashioned kettle she had got into the habit of using on the range rather than rely on the eccentric habits of their generator.

'Worth it, though. Something wrong?' he queried when Catriona gave him a rather preoccupied smile. 'Magnus isn't worse, is he?'

'He's gone out for a walk.' Catriona worried about these solitary walks of her brother's, with only his dog for company. 'Mac, we had a letter this morning. They want to build a back-up terminal on Falla.'

'And you're against the idea?'

She nodded.

'What does Magnus say?'

She told him, adding that she was surprised that he hadn't vetoed it from the very start, but mentioning how he had changed when she had suggested that he might do the survey.

'Umm. It could be a good sign. It proves that he hasn't withdrawn totally from the outside world. As a matter of fact, having men here from his old life might be the best thing that could happen to him. Seeing them might help him get over the mental block he's erected inside himself and drive him out of himself.'

'And if it doesn't? If it makes him withdraw even further? Oh, Mac, I'm so frightened for him! I'm sure he's only considering this terminal because he thinks it will be best for the rest of us. If you could have seen him this afternoon when he was talking about the accident. . . .'

'But don't you see?' Mac demanded, suddenly excited. 'He *did* talk about it. Who knows, this desire to allow them on to Falla might be a deeply hidden longing to return to his old life.'

'Then you think I should agree?'

He got up and came over to her, his eyes kind and understanding. 'Not just agree, Cat, but actively encourage him. Can you do that?'

She had to turn away so that he wouldn't see the despair in her eyes.

'I don't know,' she admitted. 'You know how I feel about the industry.'

'Aye, you're a bonny hater,' Mac agreed with a smile which robbed the words of criticism. 'But Magnus is right, you owe it to your people to at least let them make explorations.'

Catriona knew when she was defeated. Much as she hated the idea it looked as though she was going to have to give in, but that didn't mean that she had stopped fighting. One sign that Falla was going to be despoiled, one hint that these intruders were adversely affecting Magnus and they would be gone.

'You can't go on living like this, Cat,' Mac added gently. 'It wasn't what your parents would have wanted for you. How long is it since you last went out to a dance, or enjoyed yourself at all, come to that?' He tweaked her long braid, and although Catriona had been about to protest that she didn't mind, that she didn't miss the fun and glamour of London, she was suddenly conscious of the picture she must present in her heavy sweater and shabby jeans, and grimaced slightly.

Having persuaded Mac to stay and eat with them, and assured him that Findlay would take him back to Lerwick, she collected cutlery from a drawer and started to place it on the table. She and Magnus always ate in the kitchen; for one thing it was always warm, and that had become an important consideration in their lives.

The meal she had planned was only simple: omelettes made from the eggs she had gathered that afternoon, homemade bread, and some scones she had just placed in the oven. Magnus walked in as she was beating the eggs. His walk had brought the colour to a face which had grown unnaturally pale, and Catriona was pleased to see that he greeted their visitor with enthusiasm. As she had hoped he would, Mac introduced the subject of the proposed oil terminal, and as Catriona moved deftly about the old-fashioned kitchen the two men discussed the possible outcome if the geologists' report was favourable.

Both men praised her cooking, but Catriona couldn't help noticing that Magnus merely toyed with his food, pushing the omelette around his plate. Mac, who had been a widower for very many years, cleaned his plate appreciatively.

'Are you going to give the go-ahead, then?' he

asked Magnus as Catriona poured their tea.

'I don't see that we have much option, and at least at this stage they're only investigating.'

'Well, if you write the letter, I'll post it for you in Lerwick,' Mac offered, ignoring Catriona's faint frown. 'No point in letting the grass grow under your feet if you've made up your minds, is there now?' he commented when Magnus hesitated.

'You think they'd leave it over until spring now,' Catriona commented. 'The daylight is so short at this time of the year, always supposing the weather is good enough to allow them to get here each day.'

Mac frowned.

'But surely they'll be staying here on Falla?'

Catriona splashed hot tea on the table and mopped it up with hands that shook. This was something she had never thought of, but she saw from Magnus's face that he had.

'Come on, Catriona,' Mac coaxed. 'You can't honestly expect them to travel here each day? Where's your common sense?'

'They'll have to won't they?' she said curtly. 'Unless some of the islanders put them up.'

She cleared away their plates while the men drank their tea, and then offered to drive Mac down to the harbour when he insisted that he ought to leave. Magnus was listening to the radio and shook his head when Catriona invited him to go with them.

'He's like a hermit,' she complained as Mac helped her into the Land Rover. 'I tried to persuade him to go to Lerwick with me, but he wouldn't.'

But he had written a letter agreeing to allow the geologists to examine the voe, and it was now in Mac's shabby raincoat pocket. There were no lights to guide her along the narrow unmade road, but Catriona did not need them.

'Well, if Mohammed won't go to the mountain, have you thought about bringing the mountain to him?' Mac questioned, making her eye him query-ingly. 'You said Magnus was like a hermit,' he ex-plained patiently. 'And it isn't good for him to shut himself away like this, Cat. He's a healthy male of twenty-nine and he needs other human company. If he won't seek out that company then you'll have to bring it to him.'

'By doing what?' Catriona asked sarcastically. 'Capturing it wholesale?'

'No need to go to such extremes,' Mac chuckled, ignoring her angry glare. 'Not when you've got a ready-made solution right on your doorstep. Think, Cat,' he urged when she stared at him. 'Those geo-logists are going to need a base, somewhere to sleep and eat, and you've got all those empty bed-rooms. . . .'

The Land Rover swerved abruptly and came to a halt.

'No way,' Catriona announced determinedly.

Very gently Mac removed her hands from the steering wheel and held them in his own.

'Now it isn't very often that I talk to you like a Dutch uncle, but on this occasion I'm going to have to. What happened to Magnus was tragic, but it was an accident, Cat, no more and no less.'

'It wasn't an accident,' Catriona protested. 'United Oil knew how explosive the situation was; they could have ordered their people to leave while it was still safe, instead of which they kept them there, knowing they were in danger.'

'You're not being rational,' Mac protested. 'The

Middle East has always been explosive, and companies are responsible to shareholders, you know, they can't do just as they please. Magnus himself has no animosity. It's getting out of all proportion, Cat. I know you're bitter, and I can understand why. Don't you think it doesn't break me up inside too when I see Magnus and remember how he was? But assisting him to hide from the world isn't going to help him in the long run. He's ready to start on the road to recovery, I'm sure of it. Okay, he might never be able to go back to his old job, but the mere fact that he hasn't refused to have these men on Falla must tell you something.'

'It tells me that he puts everyone else before himself,' Catriona protested stubbornly, tears suddenly filming her eyes as she laid her head on Mac's shoulder.

'Oh, Mac, when he said they could come, I was so surprised, so full of hope, but the moment I mentioned the geologists he retreated again. He couldn't stand having them in the house—I just know it!'

'And I think you're underestimating him, Cat. It won't do any harm to give it a try, and it could do a hell of a lot of good. Just listening to them talk might help break through the barriers.'

'He'll never agree to it.'

'Then don't tell him,' Mac retorted with a promptness that told Catriona that he had been prepared for her question. 'Simply present him with a fait accompli. I wouldn't advise it, if I didn't think it was in his best interests, Cat,' he told her soberly, and Catriona knew that he meant it. He wasn't just their doctor, he was also a close and caring friend, and yet having these people in the house wasn't just totally opposed to her own personal views, it was

also tantamount to stabbing her brother in the back
with a very sharp knife.

'Fiona's coming to stay with me over Christmas,'
Mac added casually. 'She's a wee bit hurt that
Magnus continues to ignore her letters.'

Fiona MacDonald was Mac's niece, a nurse in a
large Edinburgh hospital with a sensible outlook on
life, and Catriona liked her. During their teens Fiona
and Magnus had been very close and had kept in
contact right up until the time of Magnus's accident,
since when he had refused point-blank to write to
her. 'I don't want her pity,' was all he had said in
response to Catriona's query. 'Let her keep that for
her patients.'

Now a sudden thought struck her.

'Mac, were Fiona and Magnus ever romantically
involved?' she asked curiously.

Mac shook his head.

'I don't know, my dear, but if they were don't
you think that's their business? The trouble with
those two is that they're both givers, and givers
seldom have the ability to take what they want from
life.'

Unlike her nocturnal room-mate, Catriona
thought suddenly, dismayed that she should have
thought of him. But having done so, she could not
deny that he was most definitely not a 'giver'. No,
he was quite plainly a man who took what he wanted
from life.

When she had seen Mac safely on board the yaol,
she turned back to the Land Rover, but instead of
driving straight home she stopped by the ancient
keep of the old castle and climbed out. The tower
had been a favourite haunt of her childhood. The
weathered walls were still high enough to offer some

shelter from the wind and often she had lain within their protective shelter, peering out to sea through the wind-tossed flowers. It was here that she had come when they brought the news about her parents and here that Magnus had found her, comforting her without a word being spoken.

Was Mac wrong when he claimed that the geologists' presence in their home might break through Magnus's prison walls? She knew she could not afford to take the chance that he might be, and with a heart heavy with bitter resentment she walked back to the Land Rover.

She might be forced to welcome these intruders for her brother's sake, but for herself she would continue to hate them. Not one of the men with whom Magnus had worked had made any attempt to get in touch with him since his accident; no one from United Oil had taken the trouble to come out to Falla and see him, and although Catriona would never have admitted it to her brother she was desperately afraid that when he claimed that his old companions would despise and denigrate him now, he was speaking the truth. Oilmen were hard men, without emotion or compassion, and now they were going to invade their sanctuary and spread God alone knew what havoc among them.

A fortnight went by without any response to Magnus's letter, and then a severe storm prevented the mail boat from calling, and Catriona had almost begun to think that the whole thing had blown over.

With gales blowing Mac had been unable to call, although he had spoken to them by telephone. Since her return to the island Catriona had never ceased to be grateful to her parents for installing this luxury.

'Any news about the terminal?' he enquired when he had assured himself that they were both well.

'Don't remind me of it,' Catriona begged. 'I keep hoping it will all go away.'

Mac laughed. Catriona was covered in cobwebs. She had been cleaning out the bedrooms, unearthing linen sheets from cupboards mercifully free of damp and moth. The house had been furnished long before the days of such things as central heating, when women knew how to store and cherish good linen.

Although there had been no further word from the oil company about the terminal, Catriona did not intend to be caught off guard if they did decide to go ahead.

CHAPTER THREE

THEY were another week closer to Christmas and enjoying a brief spell of relatively mild weather. The Shetlands, although not enjoying hot summers, did not experience unduly cold winters, only the wind changed, from playfulness to fierce intensity.

Catriona had been washing sheets, taking advantage of the brief daylight to get them dry and keeping an eye on them from the kitchen window. It wasn't unusual for Shetlanders to lose their washing to the sea when the wind came up, and she had no intention of letting that happen, not after having gone to all the trouble of doing it.

Magnus was in the library. Catriona heard the telephone ring and guessed that it was Mac. Magnus seemed morose later when she went in with the cup of coffee she had made him, and when her light attempts at conversation all went ignored, she retreated quietly as she had learned to do when these moods held him.

Her back was aching from cleaning floors covered in dust and washing windows that hadn't been touched in years. If she was going to be forced to endure the presence of these oilmen she wasn't going to give them the opportunity to criticise their lodgings. She had half expected Magnus to query her busyness, but he didn't even seem to be aware of it.

She had made a Christmas cake—a luxury she had permitted them because she knew that Magnus loved it—and as she lifted it out of the oven to cool she remembered that they were getting low on peat. The crofters had cut them a fresh pile enough to last them through the winter and it was duly drying, but Catriona could not carry it down to the outhouse by herself and she was reluctant to ask Magnus to help. The storm sometimes washed wood up on to the beaches, and tempted by the thought of a brisk walk she called Russet, and pulled on a shabby anorak which had once belonged to Magnus but which she now kept in the kitchen for winter forays to feed the hens and collect their eggs.

The sky was completely clear, but no Shetlander would have been deceived. They knew all too well how quickly a storm could blow up, seemingly out of nowhere.

She headed for a beach relatively close to the house where she knew that driftwood was often washed up, and parking the Land Rover on the firm strip of sand exposed by the tide, opened the door and climbed out, Russet racing round in excited circles at her heels.

The islanders used the tough Shetland ponies to carry wood and peat to their homes, and as she trudged tiredly along the beach under the weight of sea-soaked debris she had managed to gather, Catriona could not help reflecting how much easier it would have been to whistle commands to the Land Rover and have it come trotting obediently over to her.

The sea had been generous and in an hour she had managed to collect a sizeable amount of wood. The islanders still recounted with great relish the rich pickings which had once been had from the doomed Spanish Armada, as the unwieldy ships, driven before the wind, had been wrecked all along this coastline. Many still lay where they had sunk, and in summer amateur divers investigated their rotting hulls, hoping to find rare treasure in the silent depths.

Russet found a piece of wood, and obligingly Catriona threw it for him, laughing as the dog tried to chase a lingering gull and failed miserably.

On impulse, instead of heading straight back to the house she drove down to the harbour and found Findlay as she had hoped to do, busy mending lobster pots outside his croft.

'A tidy catch, but it will take some drying out,' the fisherman commented, examining the contents of the Land Rover. 'Have you no peat, then?'

'Plenty,' Catriona assured him, 'but it needs moving down off the hill, and I didn't want to bother Magnus.'

'Aye, like as not he'll be brooding over this business of the voe.'

That Findlay knew about the proposed terminal did not surprise her, and sitting on the low stone wall of the harbour, Catriona eyed him helplessly.

'What do you think about it, Fin?'

He took his time before replying—a Highland trait, although the Shetlanders were a different race from the people of the Western Isles and did not speak with their soft, Gaelic-accented Scots.

'We canna hold back progress, lassie,' he said at last. 'Time was when a young man thought himself lucky to have a fishing boat and a croft to call his own and with those he felt able to call himself any man's equal, but those days are gone.'

'Magnus says it would be selfish to deprive the people of the prosperity the terminal will bring.'

'Things must change, girl,' Findlay told her gently, reading her mind and knowing the turbulent resentment she was concealing beneath the surface. 'Have you not noticed that Falla is becoming an island of old people? We canna live for ever, and the fishing's not what it was. You must look forward to the future and not backwards to the past.' He put down his lobster basket and got to his feet. 'Davie's taken the boat out, but he should be back soon. When he comes we'll go up the hill and bring down your peat.'

'There's no need,' Catriona protested. 'Magnus can. . . .'

Findlay shook his head.

'Let him bide, lassie,' he advised her. 'Let him bide.'

On the way back to the house Catriona heard the sound of a helicopter and glanced upwards instinctively, her heart lightening as she saw the familiar colours. Mac must have been out to the oil rigs again and had decided to call in on them. The road was not good enough for her to drive too fast, and by the time she was approaching the house the helicopter was rising again. Parking the Land Rover in what had once been the stables and which now housed only chickens, she dashed inside.

The kitchen was empty, but she could hear voices from the library, and without pausing to take off her anorak she hurried into the room, thrusting open the door in eager anticipation, only to become rigid with shock and dismay at the sight which met her unprepared eyes.

Instead of Mac the room seemed to be full of strange men, none of whom seemed to be aware of her existence. Magnus was talking to them, his voice laced with a strain which brought a sheen of sympathetic tears to Catriona's eyes, her hands bunching into two protesting fists. Who were these men? What were they doing on Falla?

They were all bent over some papers on the desk, and one of them straightened, turning to stare at Catriona, his shock of red hair and burly shoulders vaguely familiar, and then Magnus saw her, the relief in his voice as he pronounced her name making her hurry to his side, her anxious questions stilled.

'Well, if someone can just show us to our quarters, we'll get settled in and make the most of what's left of the daylight.'

As though by magic a path had cleared to Magnus's desk and the man who had spoken the coolly authoritative words turned round. Catriona felt the breath leave her lungs on a shocked gasp, her feet like lead as she tried to move and could not.

'Cat, this is Brett Simons,' she heard Magnus say uncertainly. 'He's in charge of the team who've come to investigate the voe.'

'Wouldn't it have been advisable to let us know

before you arrived, Mr Simons?' Catriona demanded, emphasising the question by refusing to return his smile, and wondering at the same time how on earth she was managing to function so normally. Of course Magnus would expect her to be shocked at this sudden visitation, but he could have no way of knowing exactly how earth-shattering that shock had been. No one knew that but her, and perhaps the dark-haired man, with the coolly amused jade green eyes, whom Magnus had called 'Brett Simons'—the man who had forced her to share his bed and who had coolly and unmistakably shown her exactly how little effect her presence in it had had upon him!

Her heart had started to beat with panicky hurried movements, and she was conscious of Magnus frowning slightly at her rudeness. Magnus was a stickler for good manners and she knew her sharp words had surprised him.

'Brett telephoned this morning to warn me that they were on their way, Cat,' Magnus informed her reprovingly. 'I came to tell you, but you'd already gone out.'

'I expect Miss Peterson dislikes surprise arrivals as much as any other woman,' Brett Simons drawled placatingly, while Catriona seethed in impotent rage. Did he honestly think she needed his help to excuse her behaviour to Magnus? She only had to breathe one word to her brother of what had happened in Lerwick and Brett Simons and his men would be banished from Falla for ever. She took a step towards Magnus and then hesitated remembering Mac's words. An uncertain glance at Brett Simons' coolly watchful face told her nothing, but from the looks of his three companions it was plain that they were not used to *female* opposition to their boss's desires. Her tongue flicked anxiously over her dry lips, her heart thudding uncomfortably.

'I . . . we expected you to write to us,' she said at last, conscious of a small sigh running round the room as though there had been a collective releasing of breath.

'We were informed that with the bad weather the mailboat wouldn't be able to call, and once we had the go-ahead we didn't want to waste any time,' Brett Simons told her smoothly. 'I'm sorry if our appearance is unexpected.'

The last word brought Catriona's head up with a proud jerk, as she searched the green eyes for a hidden meaning. Was he trying to tell her that he knew how much *his* presence had shocked her? It was going to be bad enough having these men on the island at all, without Brett Simons thinking he had some sort of hold over her.

'Unexpected, but not catastrophic,' she replied lightly. A small movement from Magnus caught her attention, and Brett Simons was banished as she hurried to her brother's side, her smile warm and understanding. His face was pale, the bleak, haunted look back in his eyes, and now that she knew the reason for his withdrawn mood earlier in the day, Catriona could not help but regret giving in to Mac's urgings.

'It looks as though we interrupted you at some domestic task,' Brett Simons drawled lightly, momentarily distracting her and making her uncomfortably conscious of her shabby, borrowed anorak, and the untidy plait of fair hair lying on her shoulder.

'I was out gathering wood,' she replied shortly, anger sparkling in her eyes. Let him think what he liked, she wasn't going to be made to feel embarrassed because she wasn't all dressed up ready to play the gracious hostess. This was Falla, not some plush hotel in London.

'Gee, that's really quaint,' a young American voice interrupted enthusiastically. 'Is that one of your local customs round here, or what?'

The look Catriona turned on the unfortunate American boy could have burned holes through ice. He flushed unhappily, his gangly limbs and unlined face making her aware, too late, that he was little more than a teenager and had spoken impulsively, not meaning to sound derogatory. However, she was not going to back down now. If Brett Simons and his men were going to live on Falla, they would have to accept their way of life.

'These are the Shetlands,' she told him coldly, 'not New York. It may have escaped your notice, but no trees grow here, so if we want fires we either have to cut peat or find driftwood. We could always import coal from the mainland,' she continued sarcastically, 'but that comes a little expensive.'

'Thanks for the geography lesson,' Brett Simons cut in smoothly, 'Tex here has never been out of the States before and feels just about as at home as you would in Texas.'

Her cheeks flaming at the rebuke, Catriona gritted her teeth. Magnus was looking strained and pale and, anxious to talk to her brother, she suggested that their visitors help themselves to a drink from the cabinet, using the opportunity to draw Magnus out of the room so that she could talk to him.

In the passage she searched his face.

'They don't have to stay here,' she told him. 'The crofters. . . .'

'No.' His jaw was clenched, his mouth taut with pain. 'It's bad enough being a coward, I'm not going to be called inhospitable as well. You'd better get someone in to give you a hand,' he added as an afterthought, but Catriona brushed the suggestion aside.

'I'll manage,' she assured him, but really she knew that they could not afford to employ anyone and she was too proud to ask for help when she could give nothing in return.

'If you don't want them here, Magnus, we can always say we've changed our minds,' she started to say, when the library door suddenly opened and Brett Simons stepped out.

He was several inches taller than Magnus, who himself was six foot, and broader, with strong powerful shoulders and the body of a man used to demanding of it the sheer impossible.

'If you could show us to our rooms. . . .' he began.

Catriona gave him a cool smile.

'Of course, if you'll come this way, Mr Simons.' She was walking towards the stairs and his voice against her ear stopped her in tracks to stare angrily up at him as he murmured softly, 'Oh, Brett, please. Something tells me we're way past the formalities stage, or don't you agree?'

She longed to demand that he cease goading her and come right out and remind her of that shared bed, but with Magnus watching them she could do nothing but smile stiffly and agree.

'Cat. . . . No, it doesn't suit you. Not with those eyes. Kitten would be more like it, all bristling defiance and sharp claws. I wonder what you're like when you purr?'

'That's something you'll never find out,' she spat

at him, regretting the words the instant she saw the assessing glint in the jade eyes studying her face.

'We'll see about that,' he drawled warningly, leaving her to precede him on legs that trembled uncertainly beneath her as she led the way to the bedrooms she had prepared.

The house had sixteen bedrooms on two floors. Catriona and Magnus slept in the rooms which had been theirs from childhood, separated by the room which had once been Magnus's study, but which had been kept locked ever since the accident.

Catriona had decided to give the men rooms on the same floor, separated from her own by the room which had been their parents', and a bathroom, and now she wished she had put them on the upper floor. How would Magnus react to their constant presence in the house?

This thought was very much to the forefront of her mind as she pushed open the first door.

Brett examined it in silence, studying the double bed thoughtfully for a few seconds before saying with a smile,

'I see you haven't forgotten my tastes.'

As she took in his meaning Catriona flushed angrily.

'All the bedrooms have double beds,' she told him tightly. 'But do go on. You've been dying to bring *that* up ever since you saw me, haven't you? I'm only surprised you didn't mention it in front of everyone. Or do your men already know?' The words spilled out of her in a spate of bitterness, her anger so overwhelming that she wasn't aware of the teasing amusement leaving his eyes, to be replaced with cold contempt.

'Spending one night with me doesn't mean you

know all there is to know about me. And as for telling my men,' his eyes swept her coldly, 'I'm not the sort of man who needs to feed his ego by bragging about my sexual exploits.'

'Because on that occasion there was nothing to brag about!' Catriona shot back, her whole body trembling. 'But no doubt if there had been. . . .'

'Even if there had been it would have been of no concern to anyone apart from you or me.' He saw the disbelief in her eyes, his mouth compressing as he closed the door and said coldly, 'Well, if words won't convince you, perhaps this will.'

She moved quickly, but not quickly enough. He caught her as she reached the door, swinging her back effortlessly into arms which enfolded her like iron bars.

'No!'

Her pleading whisper was ignored, the green eyes keen and alert as they plumbed the anxious smoky depths of hers.

'I don't like the type of accusations you've just been hurling at me,' he told her pleasantly. 'Neither did I like the way you cut young Tex down to size. I'd be a fool not to know that you resent having us here, you've made it plain enough, or is it just me you resent? What are you afraid of?'

'Nothing!' Catriona stormed at him, but she knew that she was lying. Here it was again, that strange, tenuous emotion she had experienced only once before—lying in his arms while he kissed her firmly and without emotion.

'No?' There was amusement in the teasing word, and her pulses quickened alarmingly as it suddenly dawned on her that a man as experienced as Brett

Simons probably knew all about the trembling fear his touch was arousing.

'Don't touch me!' she cried suddenly, her jerky withdrawal brought to a halt as his arms tightened and her defiance was punished by a hard masculine kiss. Her lips stubbornly closed, she fought against him, and was surprised when he immediately released her. She had not thought him a man to give in so tamely, but her surprise turned to chagrin when she heard the voices outside the room, and guessed that while she had been oblivious to everything outside the room he had not.

The look in his eyes as he opened the door and watched her showing his men to their rooms reminded her of his anger when she had accused him of bragging about their night together, and her lips tightened angrily. Did he really think she was such a fool as to expect him to mention what had just happened in front of her? No doubt it would make a good joke for when they were alone, and yet the very evident respect with which the burly geologists treated her was in direct contradiction of her accusations.

Unwilling to admit herself in the wrong, she left them to settle in.

Brett's voice halted her at the top of the stairs and she turned, flushing betrayingly.

'What time will you want us to eat?' he queried calmly.

She hadn't really thought about it. She and Magnus didn't have any definitely set mealtimes, but knowing that the men would want to make the most of the brief daylight she said hesitantly,

'Whenever suits you.' She had been so convinced that they would not come that she hadn't got round to thinking about food, and now with a sinking heart

she contemplated their meagre resources. What they
had was sufficient for herself and Magnus, but these
men looked as though they ate huge platefuls of steak
and hearty cooked breakfasts. She would have to
telephone an order through to Lerwick and ask
Findlay to go across for it.

'Well, should we say an early breakfast, a packed
lunch and then a cooked meal at around six?' Brett
suggested easily.

Nodding, Catriona went downstairs and hurried
into the kitchen.

Magnus had disappeared and so had Russet, and
hurriedly checking through their stores, Catriona
unearthed some tins of minced beef she kept for
emergencies—all fresh meat had to be imported from
Lerwick and had lately become a once-a-month
luxury. Quickly peeling potatoes, she decided that
for tonight they would have to make do with shepherd's pie. She could make some potato cakes for
breakfast and there were plenty of eggs.

A tin of pineapple and some sponge pudding
mixture would make a filling upside-down cake. It
was just as well she had made bread yesterday and
there was still plenty of shortbread.

Once the potatoes were boiling she went outside
and started to remove the driftwood from the Land
Rover. Later on she would have to go down and see
Findlay about moving the peat. She would have to
light fires in all the bedrooms.

She was just dragging the last armful of wood from
the Land Rover when the kitchen door opened and
sighing with relief she called to Magnus to come and
help her. Only it wasn't her brother who relieved
her of her load, but Brett, his forehead creased in a
frown that made her heart thud out an alarmed

tattoo. What had she done to annoy him now?

'Why the devil are you struggling with this on your own?' he demanded tersely. 'Where's your brother?'

The note of censure in his voice made her eyes flash. She wasn't going to allow this unfeeling brute of a man, who would probably only laugh at Magnus's plight, to criticise her brother.

'I can manage on my own,' she told him fiercely, ignoring the sardonic twist of his lips which said how little he believed her.

'You really don't like me, do you?' he taunted. 'Why? *Is* it just because I forced my unwanted presence on you?'

'Does there have to be any other reason?' Catriona flung back. 'Not all women go for the big tough he-man type, you know. Some of us actively dislike it.'

'And what "type" do you go for? Or can I guess? To judge by the way you smother that brother of yours, you like 'em real soft and dependent.'

Her fingers itched to slap the cynical smile from his lips. How dared he speak so derogatively about Magnus? She thrust past him, almost overbalancing when he grasped her arm and said with maddening determination, 'I'll take the wood.'

The cottage pie disappeared faster than she would have thought possible. She had forgotten what large appetites outdoor work gave men, she reflected in dismay, uncomfortably conscious that although nothing had been said the men were still hungry. Magnus, on the other hand, although she had not given him a large portion, had barely touched it.

The young American, Tex, had endeavoured to engage her in conversation while they ate, but she had ignored him, making only brusque replies. These men were not potential friends. They were intruders, and she fully intended to keep them all—especially Brett Simons—at arm's length.

The moment she stood up to collect the empty plates, Tex was on his feet, offering to help her, but she brushed the offer aside coldly, hating herself with part of her mind for her ungracious behaviour and yet unable to forget the cool contempt in Brett's voice when he asked why Magnus had not helped her.

'Tex, if you can find those ordnance survey maps we brought with us, we can start making a study of the voe,' Brett said in a clipped voice as Catriona left the table. 'We'll need to make the most of the daylight, so we might as well do as much ground-work now as we can.'

'Who's gonna be doing the diving, boss?' the red-head, Alex, enquired, smiling at Catriona as she removed his plate. She didn't return the smile.

'I will,' Brett replied. 'That's something else we can do—check the diving gear. Know anything about diving in ice-cold water, young Tex?' he asked the American.

Catriona's lip curled a little as she listened to his careful and confident explanation of the hazards. Magnus probably knew more about cold-water diving than anyone else in the room, but his head was bent over his plate, as excluded from the conversation as though he were in another room.

She removed Brett's plate without looking at him, her lips compressing as he leaned back easily in his chair and drawled, 'Thanks for the meal, Catriona. Do you have a room we can work in this evening?'

If she had had warning of their coming she would have prepared one of the drawing rooms but it was too late to think of that now.

'You can use the library,' Magnus said tersely. 'I'm going out.'

'Don't let us push you out of your own home,' Brett began, but Magnus was already at the door, the faithful setter at his heels. Catriona flew after him, forgetting their audience.

'Magnus . . .' she protested. 'Don't . . .'

'I'm only going down to see Findlay,' he told her. 'He's got a bottle of malt down there he's been promising to share with me for years.'

In the comprehensive silence that followed, Catriona could feel Tex avoiding her eyes and hysterical laughter almost bubbled to her lips as she realised that the men thought Magnus was some kind of alcoholic. No doubt in their eyes it would explain his moods, and Magnus would probably prefer them to think that than know the truth.

Ignoring Tex's tentative offer to help with the washing up, she closed the kitchen door firmly behind them. There had been a look in Brett's eyes as he listened to her terse refusal which had made her feel ashamed of her curt words. Why should she feel shame? she asked herself angrily. She hadn't asked them to invade her home; to insult her and condemn Magnus.

When she walked past the library door an hour later all she could hear were muted male voices, punctuated occasionally by laughter, and she seethed mentally, infuriated by the sound. The sudden opening of the door caught her off guard, and she stepped back flushing guiltily, although she had no reason to do.

Brett surveyed her in silence, his lips curling comprehendingly as another burst of laughter filled the room.

'Go right ahead,' he commanded, thrusting open the door. 'Eavesdrop. I can assure you you won't hear your name mentioned. What is it with you anyway that makes you think you're so interesting as a topic of conversation?'

'I don't!' Catriona choked indignantly. 'I just wanted to use the phone and I didn't want to interrupt you.' It was partially true. She did want to speak to Mac and ask his advice about how to feed the men. He visited the rigs frequently and must know what they ate. It was plain that her shepherd's pie had not satisfied them.

His smile told her that he didn't believe her. 'Use the phone? Go ahead. The boy-friend, is it?'

He was watching her with narrowed eyes and Catriona had the feeling that if she agreed he would laugh derisively. In fact she felt quite sure that Brett Simons was well aware that the only boy-friends she had had had been strictly casual, and for the first time in her life she found herself bitterly regretting her lack of sexual expertise, although she could not have said why.

She could hardly confide her problem to Mac with the four men listening in, so she refused coldly, watching the amusement give way to dismissal as Brett turned away and closed the door on her.

By the time she had trudged up and down stairs half a dozen times with peat to light the bedroom fires, her legs were aching and her whole body felt tired, and yet she knew that when she did go to bed she would not be able to sleep. Not with Brett sleeping only three doors away.

She had put clean towels in each room, glad of the capacious back boiler which heated the water. That at least was no problem. Returning to the kitchen, she was just checking that everything was ready for the morning when the door opened and Alex poked his head round the door.

'The boss has sent me to ask about supper,' he said with a grin. 'First time I've ever known him delegate when there's a pretty girl involved.'

Supper! Catriona stared at him.

When he had gone she made a huge jug of cocoa and emptied the shortbread tin on to a plate. That would just have to do them, she decided defiantly, wheeling the trolley towards the library. She was just wondering whether to knock or walk right in when the issue was decided for her. The door opened and Brett stood there, hands on hips, staring down at the trolley. His plaid shirtsleeves were rolled up to his elbows, revealing the sinewy forearms with a sprinkling of dark hairs. Strangely enough this disturbingly masculine sight affected Catriona more than the knowledge of his nakedness in bed beside her, and her hands trembled betrayingly on the trolley as she mumbled hurriedly, 'Supper.'

'Supper?'

The incredulous contempt in the word made her flinch defensively. 'Take it or leave it, that's all there is,' she said tightly, determined not to let her embarrassment show. He had seen the house, surely he must realise how desperately hard-up they were. The lights flickered suddenly and she gasped in dismay. The generator had been behaving quite well recently, but she did not have the magic touch required to make it run when it did break down.

'What's that?' Brett queried as they flickered again.

'The generator, or did you think we got our electricity from the national grid?'

Her pithy retort provoked another frown, and the next minute the house was plunged into darkness.

'What's going on?' Alex demanded from the library, and the fourth member of the quartet, an Australian, swore colourfully in the longest speech Catriona had heard him make.

'Generator trouble,' Brett drawled laconically.

'Yes, I'd better go and look at it,' Catriona muttered, desperate to escape from the soft darkness enclosing them. What was the matter with her? she chided herself as she reached the kitchen, going automatically to the cupboard where they kept the emergency candles and the powerful battery torch. She knew exactly what kind of man Brett Simons was—cold, hard, and totally devoid of consideration for others, and yet whenever he came near her she found herself prey to the strangest emotions.

'I'll come with you.'

She hadn't heard him approach, and started to refuse, but he merely relieved her of the torch and held open the kitchen door with an implacable intent that warned her against further argument.

The generator was housed in one of the old stables, and Catriona felt her courage desert her as she opened the door and flashed the torch around. She had only the vaguest knowledge of what might be wrong. Magnus normally dealt with these emergencies, and had she been on her own she would simply have gone to bed and left it for him to deal with when he returned. However, having once taken a stand she could not depart from it, so she peered carefully at the stubbornly motionless machine, wishing that Brett would go away and leave her alone.

'Know what you're doing, do you?'

She ignored the dry probe, swearing briefly as she moved and dislodged her torch.

The torch was handed back to her in an impassive silence and, not far from tears, she tried frantically to think of all Magnus had told her about generators. It didn't help. She hadn't paid much attention. The silence seemed to grow and tauten, making her all fingers and thumbs, until at last she was pushed aside with a curt admonition, and an instruction to hold the torch steady.

'My God, this thing must be as old as the hills!' Brett exclaimed in in tones of deep disgust, but nevertheless his fingers seemed to know exactly what to do, and it was with a feeling of intense chagrin that Catriona heard the reassuring thud, thud of the machine as it was re-started.

'Why don't you get a new one, or is it just another way of making us feel unwelcome here?'

Catriona's lips trembled as she tried to tighten them into disdain.

'It wasn't our idea to have an oil terminal on Falla,' she reminded him bitterly.

'You haven't got one yet; perhaps you ought to remind yourself of that from time to time. If you're so against us you could always have refused. Why didn't you?' he asked suddenly.

Catriona kept silent. She wasn't going to explain to him about Magnus. He would never understand.

'I see.' Scorn laced the words. 'Well, I suppose all that money was quite an inducement, but you haven't got it yet, and you won't, if that voe isn't suitable.'

Furiously, Catriona opened her mouth to deny his accusations, then closed it again. Why should she care what he thought? It wouldn't be the first time he had misjudged her.

'Thanks for mending the generator,' she said brittly. 'You must let us have your bill.'

'Funny,' he said in a voice as cold as the winds which swept the Shetlands, 'I didn't have you down as a money-grabber. Proud, stubborn, and something of an innocent, that was what I thought. I couldn't have been more wrong, could I?'

He turned on his heel without another word, leaving her to stare white-faced after him, wondering at the pain which stabbed deep at her heart. Why was it this man seemed to have the knack of turning circumstances to suit himself; forcing her to appear in a bad light when all the time . . . Stifling a sigh, she made her way back to the kitchen. She hadn't fed the hens yet, and she had to go down and see Findlay, and Magnus wasn't back.

Half an hour later she brought the Land Rover to a halt outside Findlay's cottage. An old-fashioned oil lamp gleamed in the window, and Findlay opened the door to her with a dour look.

'Himself's over there,' he said, jerking his head in the direction of the fire. Findlay's mother had been a MacDonald from the Islands and sometimes his voice had the Highland lilt he had heard at her knee.

Catriona's heart sank as she saw her brother. His eyes were closed, his breathing harsh, and an empty bottle of whisky on the table in front of him told his own story.

'Couldn't you have stopped him?' she reproached. Findlay shook his head.

'Don't think too harshly of him, lassie. It was a hard thing for him to listen to yon men and all the time their words tearing the heart out of him.'

As she looked at her brother Catriona's expression softened. 'Help me get him in the Land Rover,' she told Findlay. 'Can you go across to Lerwick for me tomorrow? I need food.'

He frowned and pulled at his bottom lip. 'The weather is coming in bad,' he warned her. 'Can the doctor no bring the stuff out on his way to the rig?'

'I'll ask him.'

It was hard to keep the disappointment out of her voice, but Catriona knew Findlay would have gone had it been at all possible.

'I can let you have some fish,' he offered as he pulled Magnus out of his chair and draping an arm round his own shoulders started to manoeuvre him out to the Land Rover. Her brother was a dead weight and Catriona was panting by the time they had him safely installed in the front passenger seat. His head lolled unconsciously and tears stung her eyes.

'The lad will be all right,' Findlay assured her comfortingly. 'Apart from a wee headache, that is,' he added with a twinkle. 'Dinna fret about him, nor think too hardly of him . . .'

'I don't.'

She waited while Findlay loaded a full basket of fish and then turned the Land Rover slowly, taking care not to jolt Magnus too much as she drove slowly home. Her heart ached for her brother, and she wished she had never agreed to have Brett and his team on Falla. If Magnus was like this after only a few hours what would he be reduced to before they left? If only Mac were here to consult! Almost she was tempted to tell Brett to leave immediately. Her forehead was furrowed in a deep frown as she stopped the Land Rover. Magnus roused slightly and muttered something, half falling and half stumbling to the ground. Even in his present weakened state he was still much bigger than Catriona, each step an effort as she urged him towards the house. Russet whined unhappily as though unable to understand why Magnus was leaning so heavily on his sister.

By the time she had got him into the kitchen Catriona was out of breath. She thought about making some coffee and then dismissed the idea. What was the point in waking him up to lie sleepless all night? Taking a deep breath, she braced herself to take his weight and heaved him off the chair, which went crashing to the floor. Russet yelped as the chair caught his paw and Catriona shushed him. There was no sound from the library and presumably the others had gone to bed.

At the end of the hall, she paused for breath before tackling the stairs. If it wasn't for their unwanted guests she would have left Magnus to sleep it off in the library, but she couldn't leave him there for them to find.

She had managed to drag him up three stairs by grasping him under the arms and pulling him up behind her, when a sudden shaft of light alerted her to the fact that they were no longer alone.

'What the devil . . .' the incredulous words faded and a look of deep disgust filled Brett's face as he took in the scene.

'For God's sake . . .'

Catriona was shouldered aside as Brett took over from her, his grip much surer than hers as he pulled Magnus to his feet, supporting his weight with an ease which Catriona envied.

'Does he make a habit of this?' he enquired in

accents of biting contempt as he glanced into Magnus's oblivious face.

'No, he does not.'

Her tone brought Brett's eyes to her face in a look of thorough inspection.

'At least I wasn't completely wrong about you,' he drawled astutely. 'You do possess some virtues— like loyalty—although I suspect that it's to a lost cause. Which is his room?'

'This one,' Catriona told him, pushing open the door. Brett frowned dismissively at her as he dropped Magnus on to the bed and started to remove his heavy jacket, but Catriona stepped forward, her hand on his arm.

'Thank you. You can leave him to me now . . .'

'There speaks the voice of experience,' Brett goaded contemptuously. 'And yet I could have sworn that all that virginal modesty I saw was genuine.'

Catriona had no intention of telling him that she didn't want him to stay because she was frightened Magnus would come round and see him. Intuitively she knew that in his present state, the knowledge that someone other than her had witnessed his moment of weakness would destroy her brother entirely.

'Please go,' she said quietly, holding open the door, and after one brief, contemptuous glance at the prone body of her brother, Brett complied.

'Quite a pair, aren't you?' he demanded at the door, with a twisted smile, his eyes cold as Catriona drew herself up with unconscious hauteur. 'Don't bother with the act for me. I already know what you are, remember?'

And she knew what he was, Catriona reminded

herself when he had gone. An insensitive male chauvinist!

CHAPTER FOUR

SHE had set her alarm for six, so that she would be up in time to prepare pasties for the men's lunch before making breakfast. The bedroom fires had seriously depleted their low stock of peat and she had to make several journeys to the outhouse to bring in the damp wood. If she could dry it off in the kitchen it would help eke out the peat until Findlay and his brother David could bring some more down for her.

She was busy mixing bread dough when she remembered that she hadn't spoken to Mac, and she left the dough to rise while she made her call.

The metallic tones of his answering service informed her that he wasn't in, and leaving a message to tell him of their plight she hung up. Outside it was still dark, although it was nearly seven o'clock. She laid the table and went to mix the hens' mash, pulling on her old anorak as she headed for the door.

Outside the wind buffeted her, teasing the hair she had not had time to restrain this morning. The hens clucked round her as she spooned the steaming mash into the wooden trough. In summer they could forage for food, but in winter there was little for them to eat. The three geese she was supposed to be fattening for eating came waddling into the yard, and she repressed a small sigh. Something told her that

even if she could be hard-hearted enough to persuade
Magnus to wring their necks she would never be able to
touch a mouthful of their meat, which was ridiculous
and showed how soft she had grown living in London.

Even during the short space of time she had been
out the wind seemed to have increased in velocity;
proof of Findlay's claim that he would not be able
to take the boat to Lerwick.

They were well stocked up with flour and tinned
foods—indeed for their normal needs there was
plenty, but with four extra mouths to feed it wouldn't
be long before they were dangerously low. Catriona
could only hope that Mac would be able to bring
them some supplies on his way to the rig, when he
made his bi-weekly visit.

The appetising aroma of freshly baking bread was
filling the large kitchen when the door opened and
Brett walked in. Catriona was bent over the sink
peeling potatoes for the soup she intended to make
for the evening meal. Beside the sink on a wire rack
sat the pasties she had just taken out of the oven to
make room for the bread. She had made eight, filling
them with potato and what was left of the mince,
hoping against hope that they would satisfy the
men's large appetites.

For breakfast she had made potato cakes and porridge. Having seen the way they had eaten the shepherd's pie she doubted that her meagre supply of
bacon would go very far, and there were always eggs
if they were still hungry.

'Filling, but not very nutritional,' Brett commented critically, eyeing the potato cakes. 'This
might be enough for that drunken brother of yours,
but my men are used to food that's rich in protein,
not stodge.'

His criticisms took Catriona's breath away, her hands clenching into small, impotent fists as she was forced to listen to them, but uppermost in her mind was not his unkind words about her cooking, but the contempt in his voice when he mentioned Magnus.

The others came into the kitchen before she could retaliate, and she served their breakfast in a silence of cold rejection.

She had made a pot of tea and poured a cup for Magnus. He was awake, his eyes wary and unhappy.

'Shall we tell them to go?' she asked impulsively, putting the mug on the bedside table.

Magnus shook his head.

'We can't,' he said harshly. 'God, my head aches! Have we any aspirin?'

Catriona knew that the subject was closed, and after getting him some tablets from the bathroom, she went back downstairs. As she went towards the kitchen door she heard her name mentioned and froze. Alex was speaking, his voice edged with impatience.

'Even if the voe is any good,' he was saying, 'I can't see these two agreeing to the terminal—they haven't exactly given us the red carpet treatment, have they?'

'We'll deal with that problem when we come to it,' Catriona heard Brett reply in crisp tones. 'I've got my own ideas on that subject.'

'A spot of the old Simons charm, do you mean?' Alex retorted with a laugh, which the others joined in.

'Gee, I'm hungry,' Catriona heard Tex complain. 'Do you suppose these folks have ever heard of steaks?' he added wistfully. 'Back home we get them the size of this plate and as many as you want.'

Two spots of angry colour burned in Catriona's cheeks as she banged open the kitchen door. None of the men said anything to her as she deftly packed their lunches in foil, but Brett's eyes rested contemplatively on her fingers as they trembled over their task.

Magnus came downstairs after they had gone, refusing any breakfast. He went straight into the library and when Catriona took him a cup of coffee she found him poring over a map of the island. The look on his face as he saw her tore at her heart, and she knew that although he would deny it vigorously if she taxed him with it, Magnus was thinking of the voe and perhaps even longing to be out there with the men.

They returned late in the afternoon, damp and muddy. 'There's plenty of hot water if you want baths,' she informed them, flushing angrily as Brett's eyebrows rose in sardonic disbelief.

'Thanks,' was all he said, but Catriona heard Alex saying longingly, 'I could murder a drink, do you think there's any chance . . .'

'About as much as finding water in the Sahara,' came Brett's dry response. 'And if you do it will be as fiercely guarded.'

The bowls of steaming soup were cleared and Catriona served the steak and kidney pie she had made. Even with four full-sized tins of meat in it— enough to last Magnus and her a month—there was still barely sufficient to fill the men's plates, and she felt herself flushing under the grim appraisal Brett was giving her. She couldn't help it if there wasn't enough for them to eat, she thought indignantly. It

was their own fault for not warning her of their arrival. Even so she knew she had let their stores get
down too low, mainly because of their slender means,
but it was too late now to regret such modern
luxuries as deep freezers to hold a plentiful supply of
meat, and the money to buy it. She had fish for
tomorrow and Findlay had also brought a fresh
supply of goat's milk from Margaret Cullon, who
kept the whole island supplied from her small herd.
She noticed Tex pulling a slight face as he drank his
tea, and her lips tightened slightly.

'I want to go over the diving routine,' Brett announced, standing up and pushing back his chair.
'We'll make the dive tomorrow.'

'But you said we'd have to wait until the wind
dropped,' Tex protested, and as she started to clear
the table Catriona heard Bill, the Australian, saying
quite clearly,

'That was before he realised we were in danger of
dying of starvation.'

Sometimes in the evening Catriona and Magnus
played cards or dominoes, and when Magnus suggested a game Catriona was quick to agree, even
though she had planned to spend the evening preparing for the morning. It was the first time since
the others had arrived that Magnus had taken the
initiative in anything, and bravely she put the
burden of all the chores awaiting her attention
behind her as she followed him through into the
library.

Brett was sitting reading a book when she walked
in. Tonight Tex had known better than to offer to
help with the washing up, but Catriona's eyes
hardened as she looked at the four men, relaxing
while she slaved to provide food which earned her

nothing but insults. Before she could go to bed the
fires had to be attended to, the breakfast made ready,
the hens fed, and a thousand and one other small
jobs.

'Cards or dominoes?' Magnus asked.

'Dominoes. I'm not up to one of your games of
cards.'

Magnus laughed. 'We could get out the Monopoly
board if you feel like that.'

'Why not?' Seeing her brother so relaxed and
cheerful raised her spirits and she didn't even frown
at Tex, when, drawn by their laughter, he came over
to watch the game.

'Gee, it looks like fun!' he exclaimed when
Catriona crowed triumphantly as she gained the
waterworks. The old-fashioned grandfather clock in
the hall struck nine, reminding her of all she had to
do.

'If you like you can take over while I go and make
the supper,' she offered to the young American, feeling guilty at the way his face lit up. 'Magnus will
help you.'

'Say, can I really?' he breathed.

As she left the room the other men were already
glancing curiously at the board. All except Brett,
whose eyes never left his book.

At the moment life was a constant race against
time, Catriona reflected as she hurried in with some
peat. It was scones for supper, and porridge and
kippers for breakfast looked very meagre fare
indeed.

Sighing, she lugged the peat basket through the
hall and up the stairs. She had made the beds while
the men were out and she barely glanced round the
rooms as she stacked the peat and checked the fires.

She was just trudging upstairs with the last load when Brett's bedroom door was flung open and he stood on the threshold, his face dark with disbelief.

'What in God's name are you doing?' he exclaimed, his eyes going from her bowed shoulders to the fair hair falling over her face, and the unwieldy basket with its heavy contents.

'I should have thought that was obvious,' she retorted through gritted teeth. 'Or did you think the fires in your bedrooms made themselves up?'

'What I thought,' Brett countered in dangerously quiet tones, 'was that that brother of yours would attend to such tasks. What the hell does he do, Catriona? Apart from get blind drunk, of course, and play childish games? Hell, what kind of man is he to sit around and let his *sister* wear herself out while he does nothing . . .'

'A better kind of man than you could ever be!' Catriona sobbed bitterly. 'Don't you dare criticise Magnus—he's . . .'

'He's what?'

Somehow or other she had been relieved of the peat and drawn inside the room. Almost subconsciously she had left it until last, and now the sight of a discarded shirt and pair of jeans on a chair made her flush with memories of Brett's hard body.

'Well?' he prodded. 'You were about to tell me about your wonderful brother. He's got it made, hasn't he? Doesn't have to lift his finger while he turns his sister into a drudge?'

'I'm not . . .' Catriona began, but Brett grasped a handful of her hair and dragged her over to the old-fashioned dressing table, forcing her to stare at her reflection.

'Just take a look,' he demanded, 'and tell me what you see!'

Colour flared along her cheekbones. Her hair was untidy, the soft tendrils which had escaped his grasp framing her oval features, but it wasn't her hair that caught her attention, but the exhausted pallor of her skin, the mauve shadows beneath her eyes—eyes which she could not remember when she had last adorned with the make-up she had delighted to wear in London. Even her lips seemed to droop and lack colour.

'So I don't wear make-up,' she defended, purposely misunderstanding. 'Does that bug you? What did you expect? That I would adorn myself like a . . . a Christmas tree purely for your benefit?'

'You're exhausted,' he said unequivocally, his voice deadly quiet. 'What's the matter? Doesn't island labour come cheap enough for you?'

The insult caught her off guard, her eyes darkening like the bruised hearts of pansies, the pupils contracting with pain.

'I'm not tired,' she lied. 'I'm fine. Perhaps you're just not used to seeing women without their make-up. Perhaps I should wear eyeshadow and lipstick to give me some colour . . .'

'If it's colour you want, I can do that for you.'

He seemed to be in the grip of some strong anger, a muscle working warningly in his jaw, his eyes full of cold rage as his head descended to blot out the light.

At first his lips were harsh, punishing her for she knew not what crime, and then as a small whimper escaped her their pressure softened, stroking and persuasive. Something fluttered inside her, the warm pressure of his lips drugging her into mindless resistance until even the tiny voice that warned her to escape while she still could was silenced.

Something seemed to have happened to her will-power—it no longer existed, and she was soft and pliant beneath the hands which explored her back-bone and stroked over her curves, never lingering, but arousing nonetheless. So much so that she was instinctively pressing herself closer to Brett's warmth, returning his kiss with a passion that both shocked and exulted her. Brett's lips left her mouth to tease her earlobe, her small moan of protest alien to her ears as his thumbs stroked her throat, his eyes narrowed and lazy. Her own eyes opened hazily, bemusement very plain in their amethyst depths.

'Take a look at yourself now.'

The words brought her back to reality. Brett was releasing her to stand her in front of the mirror. Where her lips had been pale now they were rosily red and slightly swollen and her fingers trembled against them, the image shivering under her sudden rush of tears. She had been vulnerable, and Brett had made use of that vulnerability.

'All right, you've had your fun,' she said bitterly, in a voice that trembled betrayingly. 'All part of the softening up process, I suppose. Well, don't bother to waste your time—neither Magnus nor I are going to agree to this terminal unless we're quite sure that it's in the best interests of the islanders.'

'Very philanthropic,' Brett sneered. 'But I don't believe you.'

Catriona went very still, her face almost devoid of colour. 'Then believe this,' she said softly. 'I won't be persuaded by a few cheap kisses.'

It was only later, when she was in bed, that she let herself think about the emotion which had suddenly sprung to life at Brett's touch. It would be easy to tell herself that it was nothing, mere sexual attraction that would easily die, but deep down inside her she knew that it was more; much more. No man had ever affected her as Brett did, and it was her misfortune that when eventually she did decide to fall in love she had chosen a man to whom such an emotion was as useless and alien as sea water to a man dying of thirst. A tear trickled down her cheek, swiftly followed by another. She had Magnus to think of, she reminded herself fiercely. Much as she longed for Brett to simply disappear from her life, and leave her with whatever shreds of pride she had left, for her brother's sake she must pray that he did not.

The moment she awoke she knew something was wrong. For one thing it was light, and for another . . . She stared disbelievingly at the cold cup of tea beside her bed, and the alarm clock which had never been set. How could she have done such a thing? She had overslept! She raced to the bathroom, washed quickly and pulled on her jeans and sweater. Magnus was still asleep and she wondered uneasily where the cup of tea had come from. As she neared the kitchen her spirits dropped even further. She could hear sounds of laughter and smell frying bacon. Her precious store of bacon which she had meant to use for egg and bacon pie for the men's lunches. The lunches! She pushed open the door, unnerved by the silence that greeted her. A huge pile of toast sat on the table, and Brett was standing over the fire, manipulating her large frying pan on the hot plate. Without looking at her he lifted the bacon deftly from the pan, placing it in the warming cupboard before breaking eggs into the hot fat. As she counted them Catriona's eyes widened.

'Want some?' he enquired smoothly, betraying that he had been aware of her presence.

She was clutching the table for support, so great was her anger, and yet when she spoke her voice sounded calm, almost detached.

'You've used all the bacon.'

'Have I?'

His unconcerned air fractured her false calm. Drawing a ragged breath, she said bitterly, 'Yes, you have, and I was going to use that for your lunch.'

'Were you indeed? What culinary marvel was that going to be, I wonder? You're not a vegetarian by any chance, are you?'

'Isn't my cooking good enough for you?'

There might only have been the two of them in the room, so total was Catriona's concentration.

'Oh, the cooking's fine, the content leaves a lot to be desired though. Has no one ever told you about meat?'

'So what am I supposed to do? Go and ask the nearest butcher for half a dozen juicy steaks? Only one thing wrong—he happens to be in Lerwick!'

She fled the room before she broke down entirely, too tired to think of anything apart from how she was going to provide them with lunches. It occupied her thoughts to the exclusion of everything else, even when the library door was flung open and Brett, menacing and dangerous, loomed over her.

'It may have escaped your attention, but my men need proper food, they also like the occasional drink, and God knows the accommodation allowance we're paying you is generous enough.'

Accommodation allowance? Catriona stared at him. What on earth was he talking about?

'What is it with you two anyway?' Brett continued angrily. 'Or is it plain greed? That brother of yours . . .'

'Don't you dare criticise Magnus!' Her voice broke on the words, but she was past caring. 'Don't you dare sit in judgment on my brother! And as for your meals—what did you expect? This isn't a gourmet's retreat, you know.' The scorn in his eyes made her want to lash out wildly, to hurt his as his cruel words had just hurt her. She had done her best, hadn't she? Tried her hardest? Her back ached from carrying peat, her hands were sore from being constantly immersed in water; Magnus was on her mind constantly, her nerves rubbed raw from fear on his behalf, and now Brett Simons was daring to act as her judge and jury just because he and his men had had to do without fresh meat for a few days. How did he think the islanders lived?

'And while we're on the subject,' he continued coldly, taking a step towards her, 'lay off young Tex. Or did you think I hadn't noticed the way you're continually slapping him down? The poor kid's probably homesick. This is his first job, and it's not his fault that you're too mean to feed us properly.'

He was close enough for Catriona to feel his body heat, fuelled by his growing anger. So much understanding for the young American and so little for Magnus and her, she thought bitterly. Pain made her reckless and she flung at him defiantly,

'No one's asking you to stay on Falla; you can always leave.'

Her breasts were heaving with anger, Brett's eyes fastening on the betraying movement, and all at once Catriona was frighteningly aware of his maleness, of the taut fury he was controlling. His fingers grasped her shoulders, forcing her forwards until her breasts were brushing the brushed wool of his shirt, the brief contact sending awareness flaring through her, turning her anger to a breathless desire that shocked her with its intensity. Her eyes clung to the tanned column of Brett's throat above the plaid shirt, as she willed herself not to betray her feelings.

'So that's it, is it?' Brett said softly. 'All this starvation bit and lack of welcome is all designed to make us want to leave, is it? I wonder why that should be? You were keen enough on the idea before you knew that *I* was leading the team. What's the matter? You can't possible be frightened that big brother might want to leap to the defence of your honour if he discovered about our sleeping arrangements in Lerwick, because he just isn't capable.'

The insulting words banished her aching desire, her eyes flashed fire; as bleakly grey as granite cliffs. The instinctive movement of her hand towards Brett's face was stilled as he grasped her wrist, the pain bringing tears to her eyes.

'Oh no, you don't!'

She tried to escape, but her agitated movements merely brought her closer to his hard body, her breasts crushed against him as his arms clamped round her.

'So why are you so anxious to get rid of me? Or can I guess? You don't want to be reminded of the night you were forced to share your virginal bed with a brute male, is that it?'

Catriona shrank beneath the ugly note in his voice, genuinely frightened for the first time. During their previous quarrels Brett had always had himself well under control, but now she sensed that that control had gone, his eyes were burning with a fury that stripped away her thick sweater and jeans, laying bare the flesh beneath to his punishing gaze, and she trembled in fear beneath it.

'Well, perhaps it's time you learned exactly how brutal a man can be when he's pushed too far,' he gritted at her. 'Perhaps I ought to give you a concrete reason for wanting to get rid of me.'

His lips fastened on hers before she could protest, making no allowances for her tender flesh, his hand pushing aside her jumper to find the soft well of her breast.

Her gasped protest went ignored, the impotent pummelling of her fists against his chest stilled as her wrists were captured and held behind her back, leaving her with no form of protection against his leisurely exploration of her body. No man had ever touched her with such intimacy, and it didn't help to know that beneath her outrage her pulses leapt in instinctive response even while she fought stubbornly against him.

Her resistance brought only fresh pain, the angry pressure of his kiss forcing her lips back against her teeth until she could taste the salty tang of blood on her tongue, the little nip he gave her bruised skin forcing her mouth to part and endure the bitter savagery he was inflicting.

She heard footsteps outside the room with a mingling of relief and fear, staggering back against the wall as Brett released her abruptly. He was breathing hard, his eyes dilated.

'You asked for that,' he told her thickly. 'And right now you should be thanking your lucky stars I stopped when I did.'

The door swung open as he reached for it, and Catriona saw Mac's familiar features through a blur

of tears. Her first instinct to run straight into his
arms was quelled as she saw that he was looking
tired and concerned.

'The geologists have arrived then, I see,' he commented when Brett had left. 'How are you getting
on with them?'

'They're complaining that I don't give them
enough to eat,' she replied lightly, not wanting to
burden him with the truth. 'Is something wrong,
Mac?'

'My assistant's got glandular fever and things are
a bit hectic. I can't stay long, I'm on my way out to
the rig, and they're waiting for me. Cat, my dear,
you're looking tired. You aren't trying to cope all on
your own, are you?'

His kind concern brought fresh tears, hurriedly
suppressed.

'What option do I have? I can't ask someone to
work for us for nothing. Did you bring me any
supplies?'

'Oh, my dear, I'm sorry, but I couldn't. The
'copter was overloaded as it was. How's Magnus
taking things?'

Quickly she told him about Magnus's drinking,
asking anxiously if he thought it would be better to
ask the men to go. 'He seems worse, not better,' she
told him unhappily, 'and . . .'

'And what?' he prompted gently.

It was a relief to unburden herself to someone.
'It's Brett Simons, the man in charge; the one who
was here in the library. He saw me bringing Magnus
home when he was drunk. Oh, Mac, he's so contemptuous, so uncaring! Magnus is already so vulnerable . . .'

'Give it time. And about getting some help . . .

Would it assist if I made you a small loan?' Mac smiled ruefully when he saw her expression. 'Forget I said it, but you can't go on like this, Cat. You'll make yourself ill. Why don't you simply explain? I'm sure the construction company would be glad to make some contribution towards the men's expenses.'

'Brett Simons mentioned an accommodation allowance, but I don't know anything about it. We haven't had any mail for three weeks . . .'

'Then ask him to find out what's happening,' Mac urged.

Ask Brett Simons for help? She'd rather die!

'Look, I must go. I'll ring you tonight and see if there's any way we can get some stuff out to you.' He frowned anxiously. 'The construction company ought to have organised all this for you. They must know that these islands aren't geared for sophisticated modern living.'

When he had gone Catriona wandered into the kitchen, examining the larder with growing dismay. Brett had used up their supplies with a vengeance; she was down to two tins of mince, potatoes, eggs, and flour. With sick certainty she knew that her pride would not allow her to give the men shepherd's pie again. Brett Simons wanted meat, did he? Well, he would have it, if she had to die in the attempt!

She set out in the Land Rover before she could change her mind. There was no sign of Findlay when she reached the harbour, for which she was thankful, for one look at the sullen, heaving seas assured her that the fisherman would have instantly vetoed her plan. Morag James, Findlay's sister-in-law, was sitting in her window, spinning wool, and called to Catriona through the open door as she hurried past.

'Findlay's up on the hill,' she told her. 'Shall I give him a message, lassie?'

Catriona shook her head. The wind had dropped, but she knew it was only a temporary respite. The swell had an oily quality that warned her of the gale threatening. Taking her courage in both hands, she told Morag what she intended to do.

'You're no taking yon boat out in this?' Morag demanded, watching Catriona don her oilskins. 'Lassie, you canna!'

'I have to, Morag,' Catriona said firmly. 'I'll be all right. I've been out in worse than this.'

Before the old woman could voice any further doubts Catriona hurried across to the old yaol and untied the boat, thankful when the outboard fired first time.

Once out of the tiny harbour the waves crashed mercilessly down on the exposed deck, soaking her protective oilskins. The wind picked up, with a keening howl which grated on her nerves, and Catriona noticed with a tiny thrill of fear that the sea was ominously clear of gulls. The jagged-toothed rocks which marked the deep water channel were barely visible in the lashing spray; sea and sky a single grey emptiness as Catriona relied on instinct and memory alone to guide the small craft between the treacherous rocks and currents.

As the wind gathered momentum and the small boat wallowed protestingly in the storm-lashed seas she began to think she would never reach the safety of Lerwick. And all so that Brett Simons could eat meat! She checked hysterical laughter, fighting against a sudden swift current which caught at the yaol, and then, just when she was beginning to think she had drifted off course, the familiar outline of the main island and Lerwick's harbour emerged through the salt spray.

Her first port of call was the bank, where she drew out as much of their slender reserve as she dared. It vanished all too quickly as she stocked up on essentials, adding what seemed to be a huge mound of fresh meat and vegetables at a price that made her blench. Drinks were added to her purchases, her mouth bitter as she handed over the last of her money, but at least Brett Simons would not be able to accuse her of parsimony again.

She laboured under the strong wind back to the harbour, heaving a sigh of thankfulness when she reached the yaol. Carefully placing her purchases down, she was just about to start transferring them to the boat when she saw a familiar figure bearing down on her, his face tight with an anger that sent fear spiralling along her spine.

CHAPTER FIVE

SHE refused to give in to her first instinct, which was to run, and instead worked calmly to load her provisions into the boat.

She was just lifting the last box when one booted masculine foot was placed firmly on it, and her eyes were forced to travel along the lean muscled length of male thigh, and further, to the jade green eyes staring so furiously and disbelievingly at her oilskin covered figure.

'Brett! What are you . . .'

'No questions,' she was told curtly as Brett swung the box into the boat and followed it with the male bulk of his body. 'We can talk later. For now let's just concentrate on getting ourselves back to Falla in one piece, shall we?'

Catriona could only stare helplessly at him as he started the outboard with practised ease. There was something different about his anger; something dangerous and explosive that warned her that to provoke a quarrel now would be like applying a match to explosives.

Brett made no attempt to take the wheel from her, studying her with arms folded across his chest as she manoeuvred the small boat out of the harbour and into the open sea.

'How . . . how did you find me?' she asked hesitantly, when the taut silence continued to press tensely down on her. She regretted the question the moment it was uttered, smacking as it did of a deliberate intent to flee from him. Anger flared momentarily in his eyes before he spoke, in a voice cutting with disdain.

'It wasn't difficult; Lerwick isn't exactly awash with females stupid enough to put to sea in such hazardous conditions; but then you're attracted to danger like a magnet to metal, aren't you, Catriona?'

She wasn't able to answer; a wave caught the yaol sideways on, making her wallow heavily in the current which was trying to sweep them against the jagged rocks rising from the sea like serrated-edged teeth. Her heart in her mouth, Catriona battled for control of the small boat. The sudden warmth against her back told her of Brett's presence; his hands next to hers on the wheel helping to bring the yaol back on course. When she was sure that they had escaped the current, Catriona turned to thank him shakily, knowing that without his strength the boat would have been swept on to the rocks and ripped apart.

'For what?' Brett responded sardonically. 'It was in my own interests, after all. I don't intend to die for the sake of a piece of steak.'

It was his first reference to the purpose of her journey and Catriona's heart leaped uncomfortably.

'How did you know I'd gone?' she stammered hesitantly.

'I saw the boat. You caused quite a panic. Magnus was nearly out of his mind—and Findlay. I called up the rig and had them bring me out here in the 'copter. Why didn't you explain to me about Magnus?' he demanded softly, transfixing her with the unexpectedness of the question. 'And the money? Why didn't you tell me about that either, or can I guess?'

'I'm sure you already have done,' Catriona heard herself replying in a voice far removed from her normal soft tones.

'Oh yeah! I'm sure it must have given you quite a kick to keep me in the dark; letting me think that you were deliberately trying to make us uncomfortable when all the time you simply couldn't afford to feed us. You must have really enjoyed making me into the biggest heel of all time. And Magnus, you liked letting me think he was a drunken idler, didn't you. Why?'

'I didn't think you'd understand.' Her brain was whirling in confusion. How on earth had he found out so much? Surely Magnus hadn't told him, nor Findlay?

'That wasn't the explanation I got from Mac,'

Brett said quietly, so quietly that at first she wasn't sure she had heard him correctly. 'He was in the 'copter when they came to pick me up,' he added conversationally, as though they were discussing nothing more important than the weather. 'We had quite an interesting talk.'

There was menace underlying the words and Catriona's mouth had gone dry. She was grateful that the yaol demanded her full attention because that meant that she didn't have to face Brett.

'Did you really think I was the sort of man to pour contempt on Magnus simply because he was the victim of circumstances completely outside his control?' he demanded with sudden savagery. 'God, you know where to stick the knife in where it hurts, don't you? Don't you know that what happened to Magnus is the nightmare that haunts all of us? Did you really think me so lacking in compassion, in human feeling, that I would have scorned him? Is that how you see me? A man without finer feelings, totally insensitive, a male animal and nothing more?'

'Magnus didn't want anyone to know.'

'That I can understand—and appreciate—but we're not talking about his feelings, we're talking about yours. About your assessment of me—a damned insulting assessment. Mac says you've got a chip on your shoulder about oilmen,' he said abruptly. 'Is that true?'

'Are you asking me, or telling me?' she countered bitterly. 'It seems to me that I'm not the only person round here who's been making assessments. You sweep into our lives, judging us without knowing us, deriding Magnus—do you honestly wonder that I wanted to protect him from you? Mac had no right,

no right at all to tell you what he did!' she finished
jerkily, barely aware of her hands being removed
from the wheel, and Brett's taking their place, so
that she was trapped in the circle of his arms and
immediately consumed with a longing to lay down
the burdens of her cares and lean back in Brett's
arms, safe and protected. For one unguarded
moment she let herself dream of how it could have
been had Brett felt about her as she felt about him.

'Mac told me because he thinks I can help
Magnus, and so do I,' he told her arrogantly.

'Help him?' Her sudden movement jerked the yaol
off course, but Brett had the boat under control.

'Why should you?'

'Because I'm a human being,' Brett announced
grimly. 'Because I could so easily have been in your
brother's shoes. Because it's man's natural instinct to
help his fellow man. You enjoyed hating me, didn't
you?' he demanded, suddenly changing the subject.

Hating him? If only he knew!

When she remained silent, he smiled sardonically,
their only other conversation his curt queries to her
about the currents and hazards as he manoeuvred
the small boat far more ably than she had done herself back towards the safety of Falla.

They were just outside the harbour when the yaol
was caught in a fierce crosswind.

'Look out!' Brett shouted warningly to Catriona
as the huge wave crashed down over their un-
protected bows, but the warning came too late, and
it was only the firm grip of Brett's fingers that prevented her from being swept overboard by the
seething sea.

Drenched and shivering, she was hauled unceremoniously into his hard arms.

'Thank you.'

The words were stammered between chattering teeth, and as Brett's eyes swept her Catriona was suddenly conscious of her bedraggled and damp appearance.

'Hurt, did it?' he asked succinctly. 'Having to thank me?'

What hurt was that he was treating her with indifferent scorn, while all she longed for was to be held in his arms and never set free.

Much to her surprise there was no one by the harbour to greet them. Brett took over immediately, commanding Catriona to sit in the Land Rover, while he loaded the boxes, mercifully still dry under their protective tarpaulin.

By the time they were ready to leave Catriona was shivering in her damp clothes, small pools of sea-water forming at her feet. Brett gave her one comprehensive glance before putting the Land Rover in gear, the anger in his eyes making her tremble inwardly in dread of the unleashing of that anger against her.

When they reached the house she pushed open the Land Rover door without waiting for him, staggering to the kitchen against the buffeting wind. The fire had burned low, and the house seemed empty, even though it was already dark outside.

She was struggling to place fresh peat on the fire when Brett shouldered open the door and dumped a box of groceries on the table.

'What the . . .'

The peat was wrenched out of her hands with a force that sent her spinning back.

'You just can't stop, can you?' Brett grated. 'You're in no condition to heave this stuff about, or have you forgotten that you were all but swept out to sea back there?'

'I've thanked you, haven't I?' Catriona muttered jerkily. 'What do you want, blood?'

Her clothes were clinging wetly to her body and she was shivering badly, but somehow it seemed more important to go on defying Brett than to give in to the tremors racking her. She bent down to retrieve the peat, caught off guard when, with a sudden curse, Brett reached for her, swinging her up in his arms, despite her commands to be set free.

As he strode past the library she heard the muted sound of voices and prayed that the others would not emerge to see her being carried so unceremoniously upstairs.

Brett pushed open his bedroom door without checking, pushing her into a chair while he added peat to the fire. She started to protest, but felt too weak to do what her brain was urging her to do, and walk out of the room.

'Drink this.'

A glass of amber liquid was thrust into her hand, then removed impatiently and tilted forcefully against her lips. She cried out as the fiery liquid stung her cut flesh, flushing as Brett's eyes narrowed.

'Did I do that?' he demanded tersely, his fingers touching the lacerated flesh.

His touch was like balm to the wounds, and she trembled convulsively, longing for him to prolong the contact and yet fearful of the outcome if he did.

'You're soaking!'

The rough words brought her back to sanity.

'Yes. I must go and change. The men will be wanting their meal.'

'Stay where you are.'

The terse command silenced her. Brett moved over to a cupboard and removed a thick, fluffy towel, while Catriona watched him with bemused eyes. What was he going to do?

She soon knew. Without giving her time to protest he bent over her, turning her chair towards the fire, his fingers curling into the hem of her damp sweater, and pulling it upwards to reveal the clinging scrap of lace moulding her breasts.

Her gasp of alarm was lost in the heavy folds of the damp wool as he pulled it mercilessly over her head, his fingers busy with the waistband of her jeans while she was still bemoaning the loss of her sweater.

'I've seen it all before, remember,' was his only comment when she tried to stop him removing her soaking jeans. 'It's high time someone around here started looking after you.'

She was lifted up and wrapped securely in the huge towel, as effortlessly as though she were a child. Warmth was restored to her chilled flesh as Brett rubbed her briskly dry. With a growing sense of shame Catriona acknowledged that while Brett's touch was completely impersonal her own response to it was that of a woman to her lover. The spirit he had made her drink was making her feel deliciously vague, as though she were floating on a cloud, a world away from all her problems and worries. She lay passive and obedient as Brett continued his ministrations, a secret smile curving her lips as she studied his features; the full, sensual curve of his lower lip, the thick dark eyelashes, far too luxuriant to be wasted on a man; the sharply defined cheekbones and tanned flesh. She ached to touch him; to wind her fingers in the springy darkness of his dark hair; to draw him close and feel the warm possession of his lips.

She was barely aware of the brisk towelling motion ceasing; of Brett studying her newly awakened features; of his hand suddenly sliding beneath the towel to stroke and caress.

Only when he reached behind her to unclip her bra and free the swelling softness of her breasts did she look up at him, but then his mouth was on hers, warmly persuasive, and she forgot all her promises to herself not to betray her feelings. Her arms crept round his neck, her fingers stroking his nape and tangling in the thick dark hair. She was dimly conscious of being lifted, of the towel slipping away, of Brett sitting in the chair with her held firmly in his arms, the firelight playing seductively along the creamy length of her body.

She felt no shame under his open scrutiny, her heart pounding with excitement as she watched desire flare in his eyes, her body trembling in response.

'So beautiful,' Brett murmured softly, dropping light kisses on her face. 'It's a crime to hide it all under those hideous clothes.' His voice took on a deeper timbre that shuddered through her. 'If I had my way you wouldn't be allowed to wear anything at all . . .'

His eyes were eating her flesh, sending waves of heated desire burning through her.

'And then I'd freeze to death,' she replied dreamily, joining in the game.

'And I'd have to find some way of keeping you warm—like this,' Brett muttered thickly, crushing her against him so that her body felt the hard male imprint of his.

Her hands slid inside his shirt to caress the smooth muscles of his shoulders, her protest against the impeding buttons swiftly silenced as Brett muttered something, pulling the shirt free of his jeans and shrugging it off. Her sigh of satisfaction was lost against the flesh she was mutely adoring with her kisses, the hands which coaxed her breasts to burgeoning arousal taking her to a world she had never dreamed existed.

'In a moment, darling, in a moment,' Brett gasped hoarsely as she arched convulsively beneath him. 'This time we'll make proper use of that double bed, mm?'

Catriona froze, sickened by a sudden wave of self-revulsion. What on earth was she doing? It must be the whisky Brett had given her. There couldn't be any other possible explanation for her abandoned behaviour. Was this how Brett intended to make sure that she and Magnus agreed to the terminal? She pushed despairingly at his chest, shocked by the sudden icy narrowing of his eyes, as they fixed on her in cold contempt.

'What's the matter? Seeing just how far you could push me? Punishing me for daring to sleep in the same bed as you?'

'That has nothing to do with it.'

'No?' He watched her sardonically while she pulled on her still damp clothes.

'Why do you persist in keeping me at a distance, Catriona?'

'Perhaps because I know your motives for wanting to get close to me.'

'Oh?' He had gone very still, his eyes as hard as malachite as he watched, 'And just what might those be? he asked softly.

She wasn't going to back down now, Catriona told herself. For a few minutes in his arms she had been in heaven, but she would be deluding herself if she thought the bliss she had experienced was anything other than transitory. Brett wanted her goodwill, and he didn't care how he went about getting it.

'I heard you telling the other men that there were ways of getting round Magnus and me.'

'Did you indeed?' His voice was silky-smooth with contempt. 'Am I to take it that you draw the line at expecting me to use the same methods on Magnus, or do I presume that you consider there are no limits to my vileness?'

He was pulling on his shirt as he spoke, his mouth taut with anger.

'Get out of here,' he ordered, thrusting open the door. 'If you ever manage to get rid of those blinkers you're wearing you could turn out to be quite a woman, but somehow I doubt that you'll ever make it. Until you start learning to trust other people, you're going to spend your life looking for ulterior motives behind every word anyone speaks to you. At least your brother has a reason for his phobia. What excuses have you got, Catriona?'

'It won't work, Brett,' she replied in a low, pained voice. 'We both know you've *got* an ulterior motive.'

His mouth compressed in a grim smile as she walked towards the door.

'Thanks a lot,' he drawled sardonically as he held it open for her. 'You've probably just saved me from making the biggest mistake of my life.'

As she walked into her room she couldn't see for tears. Was that how he thought of making love to her? The biggest mistake of his life?

Much as she longed for the release of giving way to her emotions, she could not afford to do so. She

had five men to feed, and a house to run, and dab-
bing her eyes with cold water, she applied a trace of
eyeshadow to conceal the tell-tale traces of her tears.

The steaks were thick and juicy and even Magnus
commented appreciatively on them when Catriona
served them with crisp french fried potatoes, tiny
button mushrooms, and a delicious green salad.

She had brought fresh fruit for dessert, and Tex
sighed appreciatively as she removed their plates and
placed cheese and biscuits on the table.

'Say, that sure was some meal!' he commented
enthusiastically.

Catriona forced a smile. Brett hadn't looked once
at her during the entire proceedings.

'I'm glad you enjoyed it,' she replied automatically.

There was a different atmosphere round the table
tonight; the men were making an obvious effort to
include Magnus in their conversation, and although
he seldom spoke, Catriona was aware of the thin
film of colour on his cheekbones and his increased
appetite. She suggested serving coffee in the lounge,
thanking Tex gently when he asked if he could help
with the washing up. She hadn't missed the fresh
stack of peat by the back door and suspected that
Brett wasn't the only one who knew of their problems. If she hadn't known of his ulterior motives she
would have been so grateful to him. Her hands
trembled as she pushed the trolley into the hall. Tex
opened the door for her. She started to pour the
coffee, her hand jerking betrayingly as Brett strolled
towards her. As he reached for the cup she was
handing him, his arm brushed her breasts. Dull
colour spread under her skin, her legs trembling
uncontrollably.

'Are you all right, Cat?'

The ring of the telephone prevented her from having to answer. Mac's cheery voice greeted her, the doctor apparently not one whit disturbed at having betrayed her confidence.

'Do I still have my standing invitation to spend Christmas with you?' he asked.

'You do—although you don't deserve it,' Catriona replied dryly, knowing that she could not make any reference to Brett with everyone in the room.

'It was for your own sake, Cat,' Mac said seriously. 'And Magnus's. I don't know where you got the idea he would despise Magnus. He was most understanding. In fact he was keen to do all he could to help the both of you.'

So that they would tamely agree to the terminal, Catriona thought bitterly, unable to voice her thoughts.

'Fiona's spending Christmas with me, is it okay if I bring her along?' he added.

'We'll look forward to seeing her,' she assured him truthfully.

She was just about to hang up when Mac added startlingly, 'Did you know that Brett Simons owns the construction company chosen to build the terminal? Quite an achivement for a man who started out as a civil engineer.'

Catriona's hand was shaking when she replaced the receiver. Here was proof—if she had needed it—of Brett's duplicity. No wonder he was anxious for the terminal to go ahead! Her mouth curved derisively, making Magnus frown and ask if everything was all right.

'Fine,' she assured him with brittle emphasis. 'That was Mac. He's bringing Fiona with him when he comes for Christmas.' She looked at Brett. 'I expect you'll all be leaving us soon. You'll want to spend Christmas with your families.'

'The others will. I don't have a family to spend it with,' he replied coolly. 'If it's all the same to you, I prefer to stay on. I want to be through here as quickly as possible. We'll pay you extra, for the inconvenience, of course.'

He couldn't have been more distant or cold, but then of course now that she had seen through him he had no need to turn on the charm for her, Catriona thought bitterly. There had been a faint emphasis on his claim that he wanted to be finished quickly which had not been lost on her.

To her surprise it was Magnus who answered him, assuring him before Catriona could speak that he was more than welcome to stay.

'It's a pity we don't have a more detailed map of the island,' Brett commented when he had thanked Magnus. 'I'd like to know a little more about that voe before I start diving.'

Brett had been talking to Alex, but Catriona's eyes had gone instinctively to the desk where Magnus kept his maps, and as though sensing her train of thought her brother said awkwardly, 'I have some maps, I don't know if they'll be any use . . .'

An hour later five male heads were poring over the maps spread out on the desk, Magnus's voice, more assured than Catriona could remember hearing it in months, offering comments as the men discussed the terminal.

'Say, you know a real lot about this island,' Tex commented admiringly at one point, and Magnus withdrew into his shell immediately, standing up and saying that he was going to bed, but the wall behind which he had hidden himself had been breached, and it was with bitterness that Catriona was forced to acknowledge that Brett had achieved more in a day than she had managed in months.

When she started to collect the coffee cups, he grasped her arm, his eyes like flint as he challenged comprehendingly,

'Hating my guts because I managed to get Magnus to emerge from his shell? It's only natural for a man to crave the approval of his peers.'

'His peers! He wouldn't think you that if he knew why you were trying to get through to him.'

He released her without another word. In the kitchen she washed up listlessly, conscious of the deep ache inside her which had been growing all evening. Her bones turned fluid as she forced herself to re-live those moments in Brett's arms, the look in his eyes as they devoured her naked body. He had wanted her! But only momentarily, she reminded herself. That was all.

Catriona hadn't realised until she heard them discussing it over breakfast that Brett was actually going to dive into the voe that day. The wind had dropped and the forecast was reasonably good, but even so fear clutched at her heart as she contemplated the icy waters of the fiord.

'We could do with another man,' Brett commented with a frown. 'Tex here isn't used to cold water diving yet, and I want Alex to come down with me, so that means there'll be no one up top to monitor things if you two are keeping an eye on Alex and me.' He looked across the table at Magnus, his frown deepening. 'You know the area well. Have you ever swum or dived in those waters.'

Catriona held her breath as she waited for Magnus to reply.

'A bit.' The clipped accents didn't betray how much it had cost him to reply.

A bit—what an understatement! Catriona thought, remembering the summer Magnus had spent exploring that whole coastline with the aid of some old diving gear he had bought. She had pleaded to be allowed to try, but he had refused, relenting only enough to teach her the rudiments of diving. He had always been so careful of her safety.

'Would you mind giving us a hand, then?'

There was no way that Magnus could refuse the outright request. He struggled for a moment to formulate some excuse, and then, as though recognising the futility of it, shrugged his shoulders and agreed.

He looked like a man facing a firing squad, Catriona thought compassionately. He had no idea that Brett and the others knew all about his accident, and she had to bite her lip to prevent herself from telling him. White-faced, he left the kitchen and returned wearing climbing boots, thick cords and a padded weatherproof jacket.

'Well, if everyone's ready? Will it be okay for us to use your Land Rover?' he asked Catriona distantly without looking at her.

It was as though their earlier intimacy had never existed and they were complete strangers. The coldness in his eyes was like a knife in her heart, but she forced herself to respond in kind, smiling merely with her lips as she handed him the keys.

Their fingers touched, her whole body taking fire as she was swept with an impossible yearning.

When they had gone she went upstairs and made up two extra beds for Fiona and Mac. In Brett's bedroom she made up the fire with jerky movements, her eyes straying compulsively to the rumpled bed. The pillow still bore the impression of his head and like a sleepwalker she crossed over to it, her fingers running seekingly over the slight dent as tears welled and fell. His sweater was lying on the bed and she folded it automatically, the faint tang of his cologne clinging to the wool making her shake convulsively with a need which seemed to grow with every passing day. How could she survive Christmas in the same house with him?

She did not know, but somehow she must.

For dinner she was cooking a huge roast and as the daylight started to fade the appetising aroma of it cooking filled the kitchen. She was just starting to roast the potatoes when she heard the sound of a helicopter, and hurriedly finishing her task, she grabbed her anorak and rushed outside.

CHAPTER SIX

IT wasn't Mac who stepped out of the stationary craft, but two men in overalls, oil company badges sewn on the breast pockets.

'How about this for service?' one of them asked with a grin as he opened the back of the helicopter and together they lifted out a brand-new gleaming freezer. 'Where do you want us to put it, Miss?'

Catriona stared disbelievingly at them.

'I didn't order that,' she began to protest, but the men were already walking towards the kitchen and it wasn't until the freezer was standing on the kitchen floor that they spoke again.

'This is Falla, isn't it?' one of them asked Catriona, flourishing an order form. 'And you're Miss Catriona Peterson, aren't you? Brett Simons told us you wanted this thing in a hurry. There's a new generator in the 'copter too, and some supplies for the freezer. We'll bring them down for you. Now if you'll just tell us where you want us to put this thing.'

In a daze Catriona directed them towards the larder, her face taut with anger. How dared Brett do this? Anger rose inside her in a tidal wave that he should humiliate them in this fashion. For two pins she would tell the men to take the thing right back where it came from—but if she did that it would be all over Lerwick by morning. Her mouth grimly compressed, she followed the men outside. They were already manoeuvring the new generator towards the house, cheerfully offering to make sure it was running properly before they left.

From their conversation it was plain to Catriona that they had a high opinion of Brett. Well, it was one she did not share, she thought wrathfully. If he'd painted it in six-foot-high letters in the peat he couldn't have made his opinion of the meals she had been serving them more plain. She inspected the packages of food the men were depositing in the kitchen. As she had suspected it was mostly meat— lean, thick steaks, generous pieces of sirloin, huge chops, bacon, frozen vegetables of every variety, and there was even an enormous turkey. He had thought of everything Catriona, thought bitterly.

Everything but how insulting his actions were.

When the men came back Magnus and Brett were deep in conversation. Alex sniffed the air as he walked into the kitchen and asked appreciatively,

'Roast beef? With Yorkshire pudding?'

'And roast potatoes, and carrots, and sprouts,' Catriona assured him solemnly. Brett hadn't so much as looked at her, and she told herself that she was glad, because if he didn't she would not be able to contain her anger.

'So you think there's a fair chance that the voe is deep enough to take even the largest tankers?' Brett was saying to Magnus as Catriona interrupted them to ask Magnus to carve the meat.

She ate her own meal in silence, getting up as soon as she had finished to serve the apple pie. Magnus had cleaned his plate and tucked into his pie with a vigour that surprised her. The men were talking about the possibility of using explosives to deepen the voe if it should be necessary.

'I don't want to do that,' Brett interrupted firmly. 'The whole point of using Falla is that we can do so without despoiling the island.'

Without costing *his* company any extra money, Catriona thought bitterly, refusing Alex's offer to help with the washing up.

'It's my turn tonight,' Brett commented easily, getting up and walking across to the sink before she could protest. The other men went through to the library, leaving them alone, and Catriona concentrated on washing the plates with an intensity the task did not really require, determined not to address a single word to the man at her side.

It was only when all the washing up was finished and she had started to make the coffee that Brett spoke, his voice curt and angry.

'Okay, what have I done now?' he demanded.

'Do you actually need to ask?' She was quivering with fury, and acknowledged inwardly that she had been preparing for this confrontation from the moment she saw the freezer. She flung open the larder door. 'Perhaps you'd like to explain the meaning of this?'

He glanced from her bitter eyes to the gleaming freezer, one eyebrow raised in mocking irony.

'What is there to explain? I thought . . .'

'Oh, I know what you *thought*,' Catriona cut in bitterly. 'And so must half of Lerwick by now. You thought my cooking wasn't good enough, didn't you? That your precious men weren't getting enough to eat.' Her hands were clenched into angry fists as she fought against her growing sense of injustice. 'Well, we don't want your charity and we don't . . .'

'You can stop right there.'

The ice-cold words sliced straight through her angry tirade, two spots of colour burning in her cheeks as he crossed the intervening space between them in two lithe strides and shook her until she felt dizzy.

'I suppose it never occurred to you that I might have been thinking of you? That I might have wanted to make life a bit easier for you? Or did you think I hadn't seen the way you've been working yourself into the ground since we arrived?'

For a moment his exasperated words held her immobile. It had never crossed her mind that he might have bought the freezer for her! And then she remembered how much he would stand to gain if his company went ahead with the terminal and her lip curled disdainfully, contempt replacing the wavering uncertainty of her glance. Of course he would pretend he had done it for her, hoping to soften her towards him.

'Don't lie to me,' she said coldly. 'I suppose you

thought it would be easy to get round me. Well, you made a big mistake!'

'Indeed I did,' he agreed grimly, turning on his heel and wrenching open the kitchen door. 'And you think your brother's got problems!'

Leaving her to digest his comments, he slammed the door behind him.

Catriona was trembling so much that she had to sit down. Of course she had been right to suspect his motives for buying the freezer, but he was an excellent actor and for a moment she had actually experienced contrition for having accused him.

'Been playing with your new toy?' Magnus teased as she handed him his coffee. 'Brett has just been telling me about it, and the new generator. It's very generous of him,' he added warmly.

Much as she longed to tell him the truth, Catriona knew that she could not disillusion Magnus now, just as he was beginning to emerge from his protective shell. He followed her into the kitchen when she went to fill the coffee pot, full of enthusiasm for the terminal project.

'Why don't you ask them if they need any help?' she suggested casually. 'You know the sea in the voe far better than they do, and your diving kit is still outside.'

He clammed up immediately, and she regretted the suggestion. It was plain that he was still not ready to fight his conviction that he had lost his nerve.

The men were discussing the voe when they returned to the library, and Catriona couldn't help noticing the seemingly casual manner in which Brett made sure that Magnus was included in the conversation, and the way in which her brother started to let down his guard.

'It must be very interesting work,' she commented when the conversation flagged, anxious to encourage Magnus's interest.

'It is—why don't you come down and watch us?' Brett suggested, his eyes holding hers across the width of the room. 'We can always find you something to do.'

'No, thanks.' She turned away, gathering up the cups, dismayed by her reaction to his suggestion. How on earth had she managed to fall in love with a man who didn't give a damn about her? she wondered miserably.

When she had finished washing up she started to prepare for the morning and it was quite late when she finally emerged from the kitchen. She thought the others had all gone up to bed ahead of her, but as she walked past the dining room she heard someone talking, and pushed open the door.

Brett was using the telephone, his back to her, so that he was unaware of her presence.

'Come out to Sullom Voe for Christmas? Yes, I know you really push the boat out, but I can't. Umm, you could say that. There's a matter of some unfinished business and it's proving more tricky than I thought . . .'

Catriona moved slightly, and he turned, his eyes scrutinising her face. Guiltily aware of having been eavesdropping, she made a pretence of shuffling some papers on Magnus's desk and heard Brett say firmly, 'Look, Chris, I've got to go. Speak to you again.'

The receiver pinged and in the unnerving silence which followed Catriona was determined not to let him panic her into taking flight. Even so, she could not prevent herself from saying defensively, 'Don't let us stop you from visiting your friends.'

'You won't,' he assured her coolly. The look in his eyes was making her feel distinctly uneasy and she started to back towards the door, impelled by some inner fear to lash out impulsively,

'It must be very convenient having friends in such high places—especially for a civil engineer with his own business!'

'Feel happier now?' he asked succinctly. 'As it happens you couldn't be more wrong. Chris and I go back a long way and our friendship means too much for me to risk jeopardising it by asking for those sort of favours.' His eyes raked her contemptuously. 'And there's no need to cringe away from me like that. I wouldn't touch you now if you were the last woman on earth. I like my women to be *women* and not childish adolescents.'

Somehow or other Catriona managed to stumble upstairs to her bedroom, but his contemptuous words rang in her ears long after she should have been asleep. How much more agony would she have to endure before he left the island?

The morning was one of those cold, clear days of winter enchantment when the sky was clear and the wind had dropped. When the men had gone Catriona felt restless. Magnus had gone with them, and Russet whined coaxingly by the kitchen door.

'All right, but we're not going far,' she told the setter as she opened the door. Last night the men had been talking about their plans for Christmas. Tex was flying home to America, Alex was going to Dumfries to stay with his sister, and Bill the Australian was talking about going to London to some fellow exiles.

She hadn't intended to, but somehow or other she found herself walking in the direction of the voe.

From the top of the steep-sided valley she could see Magnus and Tex, tiny ant-like figures below her. A black figure bobbed up in the water, gesturing to the two others, and Catriona frowned, wondering what was going on. A second figure suddenly surfaced, clambering out of the water and pushing back the hood of his wet suit. It was Bill, and for some reason Catriona felt her stomach muscles knot with tension. Where was Brett?

The men's voices carried up towards her, but they were too far away for her to make any sense of their conversation, but from their stance, the manner in which they were watching the water, Catriona could tell that something was wrong. Without pausing for thought she was on her way down the steep slope, slithering and sliding in her haste to reach the bottom. Russet raced on ahead of her, dislodging showers of small pebbles and alerting the men down below to her presence.

'What's happening?' she demanded breathlessly when she reached them.

Magnus frowned.

'Brett hasn't come up yet. His air tanks are full, but it isn't wise to stay down too long in these temperatures.'

'I'm going down again to see if I can see him,' Alex announced, but Magnus, who suddenly seemed to have a new authority in his manner, said firmly,

'You haven't enough air. Neither of you has. Cat, take the Land Rover and go back to the house. Both my tanks should be full. Can you manage them by yourself?'

She was just about to agree, seized by a fresh sense of urgency, when Magnus added, 'Tex had better go with you to give you a hand. It will be quicker that way. Bring my wet-suit as well, will you?' he said calmly. 'As I probably know these waters better than anyone else, if anyone is going down it might as well be me.'

Remembering his claim that he couldn't dive again, Catriona stared at him, not surprised when Alex protested heatedly that if someone had to go down it was going to be him.

'We'll argue about it when Cat gets back if Brett still hasn't surfaced,' Magnus said calmly.

All the men were wearing expressions of contained urgency, so alien to their normal insouciance that Catriona's mouth went dry with terror.

'How long . . . How much air has he left?' she asked in a voice that cracked over the last words.

'By my reckoning half an hour,' Magnus told her. 'So be a good girl and get a move on.'

His calm manner stilled her panic long enough for her to climb in the Land Rover and switch on the engine, racing the machine over the bumpy ground, while Tex clung grimly to the edge of his seat.

It took her ten minutes to reach the house and Tex climbed out of the Land Rover, pale but admiring.

She didn't waste time talking; half an hour, Magnus had said, which meant that they had to load up the equipment and be on their way within five minutes if Magnus was to have any chance to finding Brett before his air ran out.

Her heart was pounding with fear as she turned the Land Rover round; her pulses racing as they urged her to achieve the impossible, thudding out the imperative refrain, 'Faster . . . faster!'

As they crested the slope above the voe Catriona

could see the men huddled round something lying on the ground. Her face as white as chalk, she glanced at Tex. His eyes mirrored her own fear and she stopped the Land Rover with a screech of brakes, stumbling towards the men.

'Cat . . .'

She barely heard Magnus, all her concentration fixed on the prone figure on the ground, lying so deathly still. Alex and Bill were bent over him.

'Is he . . .?' She couldn't formulate the words; they seemed to be stuck in her throat, her whole body tensed for the blow she felt sure must fall.

The prone figure moved and for the first time Catriona saw the smear of red against the black wet-suit. The world whirled round her and she gritted her teeth. She couldn't faint now! Alex moved and for the first time she saw Brett's face. It was as white as her own, but he was well and truly alive and the green eyes mocked her tauntingly.

'Save your ministrations for Catriona, Alex,' she heard him say laconically. 'She looks more in need of them.'

Hating him for his perception as she did, it was easy to forget that not five minutes ago she had felt that her life had come to an end. Magnus was at her side, concerned and malely impatient of her momentary weakness.

'He caught his foot in a rock crevice and cut himself pulling it free. We'd better get Mac out to take a look at it. It seems okay, but you can't be too careful.'

'Let that be a warning to you, young Tex,' Brett commented as he limped over to them. 'Don't go diving without a partner.' His eyebrows rose as he saw the diving gear in the back of the Land Rover.

'The rescue team? Who was going to use that?'

'I was,' Magnus answered curtly. 'I used to do quite a bit of diving and I know these waters.'

Still no mention of the accident or how closely connected he was with Brett's own line of work, Catriona noticed, but the mere fact that he had been contemplating diving must surely be another step in the right direction, and she was forced to admit that Mac had been right and she had been wrong.

It didn't help to know that Brett was watching her covertly as she drove the Land Rover towards the house; this time at a far steadier pace than before. Had she betrayed herself to him? Her heart pounded anxiously. A brief glance in the driving mirror forced her to acknowledge that she might have done, because he was watching her with a look in his eyes that she was unable to interpret.

'I'll get Mac on the phone,' Magnus announced when they drew up outside the house. Alex and Bill were helping Brett from the Rover, although he protested that he could manage quite well on his own.

'Mac's out,' Magnus said briefly, poking his head round the kitchen door. 'You'll have to do your first aid stuff, Cat. It's okay,' he added, grinning at Brett. 'She's fully trained. Mac taught her when we were kids. Living somewhere like Falla you never know when it'll come in handy. Even thought of becoming a nurse at one time, didn't you, Cat?'

'What stopped you?' Brett asked dryly in a voice that only carried as far as her. Despite the fact that he was very obviously in pain his eyes were still as coldly assessing as they had been when they had witnessed her betraying reaction to the sight of his prone body. 'Lack of compassion?'

She pretended that she hadn't heard him—that way she was able to contain the worst of the pain. Had he but known, he couldn't have been more wrong. 'Too sensitive and compassionate,' had been Mac's opinion when she talked to him about nursing. 'You'll break your heart over every patient,' he warned her, 'and drive yourself to a nervous breakdown before you're thirty.'

'Can you get him up to his room?' she asked Alex curtly. 'That gash will have to be bathed and cleaned.'

'I'm not dead yet, you know,' Brett interrupted caustically. 'And I'm perfectly capable of walking upstairs unaided.' Even so he leaned heavily on Alex's supporting arm as the small procession made its way slowly upstairs. Looking at his pallor Catriona was glad that the bedrooms were warm. He might be putting on an excellent front, but she had listened to Mac often enough and studied enough textbooks to know incipient shock when she saw it.

As Alex manoeuvred him awkwardly on to the bed his eyes closed, his face white beneath the shock of dark hair.

There was a comprehensive first aid kit in the bathroom and Catriona went to get in, leaving Alex in charge.

'I think he's fainted,' Alex muttered worriedly when she returned. The Scotsman's normal ebullience was notably absent and there was concern in the light blue eyes.

'Don't worry. It's only shock,' Catriona assured him. 'It was bound to happen.'

Alex himself was looking a bit green. 'Can't stand the sight of blood,' he admitted sheepishly as she opened the first aid box.

'Then you'd better go downstairs and find yourself a drink,' she told him briskly. 'I don't want two of you fainting on me!'

It was only when he had gone and the door had closed behind him that she realised that Brett hadn't fainted at all, but was watching her through narrowed eyes, his expression alert, despite the intense pain she knew he must be suffering.

'Good old Florence. Haven't you forgotten something, though?' He tried to sit up and grimaced slightly. 'Unless they've discovered a new cure-all wonder drug, won't you have to remove the wet-suit before you can clean the gash?'

His voice was very dry. In her anxiety she had forgotten all about the clinging wet-suit, moulding every muscle of a body which she now realised was in the peak of masculine fitness. With a calmness she was far from feeling she said carelessly.

'I hadn't given it much thought. If you want me to waste time and probably cause you considerable pain into the bargain by removing it I'll do so by all means, although what I had in mind was to cut it off round the wound.'

'Have you any idea how much these things cost?' he demanded dryly.

'About the same as a brand-new freezer.' She was quite proud of how calm her voice sounded. The sharp surgical scissors sliced through the rubber like butter, exposing a wound which made her grit her teeth and be grateful for the fact that Brett could not see her eyes. The gash was deep, exposing part of the bone, which mercifully appeared to be untouched. How he avoided severing an artery she did not know; the wound bled sluggishly, the torn flesh ragged as though it had been cut with a blunt knife.

'You'd better hang on to something,' she warned him as she reached for the antiseptic. 'This is going to hurt.'

'And aren't you just going to enjoy that! Do I get a sweetie and a kiss to make me feel better if I'm a good boy?' he mocked savagely.

Catriona flinched herself as she poured the antiseptic generously on the exposed wound. She was working with her back to Brett and could not see his face, but his single indrawn breath and the clenched hand lying on the coverlet told her all she needed to know. Now she realised what Mac had meant about her being too sensitive. For a moment it was as though she had felt his pain; her heart felt as though it were being wrenched out of her body, and it took every ounce of willpower to go on and cleanse the wound quickly with a fresh antiseptic dressing.

'It's going to need stitching,' she warned him. 'Mac . . .'

'Oh, for God's sake let's get it over with,' Brett demanded roughly. 'You've got needles and sutures, haven't you? Or has the thought of genuinely making me bleed lost its appeal?'

It wouldn't be the first time she had stitched up a wound, but it would be the first time she had ministered to the man she loved, and her hands shook badly as she made the neat sutures, cleansed the flesh again and applied an antiseptic dressing.

'You'll need a tetanus injection and a course of antibiotics,' she said shakily as she stood up. If anything she looked the paler of the two.

'And you look as though you need a bottle of tranquillisers,' Brett mocked, watching her dispose of the used cotton wool in the fire. As she closed up the box and walked towards the door he said softly, 'Haven't you forgotten something?'

Her head was feeling faintly muzzy. She should have covered him up, she thought hazily. He was suffering from shock and ought to be kept warm. She would get him a hot water bottle. She moved automatically back to the bed. Alex would have to help him undress, but not yet. She had put those sutures in without any anaesthetic and her own muscles had screamed protestingly over each one.

She reached for the bedcovers, tugging them down underneath him and pulling them back, her movements jerky. As she leaned forward to tuck in the sheet Brett reached for her. The sureness of his powerful grasp surprised her. Faint colour lay along the high cheekbones, and her fingers moved instinctively to his pulse.

It was racing rapidly.

'Well, nurse, what's the diagnosis?'

She ignored the mockery, looking for signs of fever. It would be natural after such an accident, but his eyes were clear and cold. She checked his pulse again and it was still fast.

'You're suffering from shock,' she told him coolly.

'Or excitement.' Green eyes held grey. 'Hasn't anyone ever told you that they both have a similar effect on the nervous system? You should try taking your own pulse after you've made love—or before,' he said softly. 'Frustration can be a mighty powerful stimulant.'

She dropped his wrist as though it were a red-hot coal. Why was he goading her like this?

'Then you'll have to find some way of relieving it, won't you?' she replied brittly. No doubt there were

plenty of girls only too ready and willing to aid him
in that direction and possibly in years to come she
would call herself a fool for not trying to be one of
them, but when you loved someone you wanted more
than merely sex.

A brooding expression darkened his eyes as they
rested on her trembling mouth.

'Perhaps I ought at that. And perhaps you'd better
get the hell out of here before I decide to find out
exactly what it takes to make your pulses race, Miss
Nightingale!'

The sound of his harsh laughter followed her out
on to the landing, where she met Alex, looking a
little less green, on his way up.

'Boss okay?' he asked, jerking his head in the
direction of Brett's room.

'He'll live.' She struggled to keep her voice light.
'He needed stitches, and I think he might be in
shock, but Mac should be here soon.'

'Shock? Brett?' Alex laughed. 'Not him. I remember once when we were in South America. He
broke his leg, and then calmly told us how to splint
it for him. That was when he decided he'd had
enough of the faraway places bit. We were fifty miles
away from anything with the remotest pretentions to
civilisation and he was damn lucky not to lose that
leg. It isn't until you come up against death that
you really start to appreciate life. Old Brett in shock
over a tiny scratch like that?' Alex laughed heartily.
'Not him!'

Mac arrived later, when Alex and Magnus between them had got Brett out of the wet-suit and
into a pair of pyjamas borrowed from Magnus for the
occasion since, as Magnus told her with a grin, their
patient did not appear to possess any of his own.

'He's a great guy, Cat,' Magnus told her while Mac was upstairs. 'The sort of man I'd have been proud to have call me friend.'

If only Magnus knew! But she couldn't wreck her brother's newly emerging self-confidence by confiding that she suspected Brett's friendship sprang from a desire to make sure arrangements for the terminal went ahead smoothly.

'Nice piece of sewing, Cat,' Mac complimented with a smile when he came back downstairs. 'The patient seems to think you suffered more than he did.' He meant it as a joke, but when Catriona blanched faintly, he eyed her curiously. No one else seemed to have noticed and when she made no response Mac said conversationally, 'Wouldn't it be better to put off any more diving until spring?'

Alex shook his head.

'No way. That would mean a wait of another twelve months before the construction work could get under way. No, Brett wants the whole thing tied up in time to start in the spring if the terminal gets the go-ahead, and from what we discovered today it looks as though it might.'

Mac drew Catriona slightly to one side on his way out.

'I can't stop now, I've got twins due in Lerwick. Magnus has improved tremendously.'

'Yes, you were right,' she admitted. 'But he's still suffering from that crippling lack of self-confidence. He's convinced the others would despise him if they knew the truth. He doesn't know you've told them.'

'I thought it wisest, Cat,' Mac said in firmly authoritative tones. 'And I made the decision as both a physician and a concerned friend. You weren't being objective about the situation. Cat, what possessed you to take the boat over to Lerwick like that? I was on the rig when Brett's call came through. I nearly had a heart attack! That was a Force Five out there and . . .'

'And so you told Brett Simons that Magnus and I hadn't two pennies to rub together, and ever since he's been treating me like Little orphan Annie. I'm sorry,' she apologised, instantly contrite, 'I shouldn't have said that. Why are you looking at me like that?' she asked, puzzled. He was regarding her with a mixture of amusement and wryness.

'I was just wondering why when you feel like that about the man you were at such pains to patch him up. See you at the end of the week. The 'copter's coming in to pick up Alex and the others can drop Fiona and me off.'

CHAPTER SEVEN

FIONA hadn't changed, Catriona thought. The other girl was like a fresh, bracing wind. They had arrived several hours ago and Fiona had immediately announced that Catriona wasn't to wait on them hand and foot, and that she, Fiona, fully intended to do her bit.

'Your lodger's quite something, isn't he?' she commented when they were alone in the kitchen. Catriona was buttering scones and bent her head over the task.

'If you like that type,' she agreed neutrally.

Fiona's eyebrows rose.

'My dear!' she exclaimed with an exaggerated drawl. 'What woman with blood in her veins wouldn't? I'm only surprised he's remained a bachelor so long. He must be in his early thirties.'

'Perhaps he doesn't believe in long-term commitments.' If only Fiona would change the subject, but she seemed to find Brett Simons positively fascinating!

'Or perhaps he's too romantic,' Fiona said shrewdly. 'His standards might be exacting, but I don't mind betting he'd make heaven right here on earth for the woman who fulfilled them.'

'You're the one who's the romantic if you think that,' Catriona scoffed. Fiona's comments lanced her aching heart like red-hot needles, and she had to thrust aside the vision they had conjured up.

Fiona looked surprised.

'Don't you like him?'

'He's not my type,' Catriona lied. 'He's far too . . .'

'Sexy?' Fiona supplied with a grin. 'As far as I'm concerned you can't have too much of a good thing. How's Magnus?' she asked, sobering up a little and changing the subject. 'Mac says he's starting to show an improvement.'

'A little,' Catriona agreed, too engrossed in her own thoughts to notice Fiona's sudden preoccupation with the trolley. 'Having the men here seems to have helped, although I was against it at first.'

'Mmm. Mac told her you were scared that the terminal would spoil the island. I can understand that, but you have to admit that the benefits would far outweigh the disadvantages.'

Brett and Fiona hit it off right away, and soon he was teasing her as though they had known one another for years; an exclusive charmed circle, Catriona thought bitterly, and one that left Magnus and herself on the outside like children with their noses pressed longingly against a sweet shop window.

'How long are you staying?' Brett asked Fiona when the supper things had been cleared away. Acutely sensitive to every nuance of his voice, Catriona wondered if she was the only one to notice how eagerly he awaited her reply.

'Until after the New Year. I had quite a lot of holiday owing to me, and this part of the world is rather special at New Year.'

'First-footing, you mean?' Brett enquired with a smile.

Fiona shook her head reprovingly. 'That's a Scottish custom. You're forgetting the Shetlanders' Norse blood. No, here at New Year they have Up-Helly-Aa, and believe me, it's really something. Remember the one you took me to three years ago, Magnus?' she enquired, turning towards him. He seemed to have withdrawn slightly since Fiona and Mac had arrived, and Catriona was worried about it.

'Vaguely.'

To cover the silence caused by the curt, dismissive word, Brett asked Fiona to tell him a little more about the celebration.

'I can do better than that,' she replied firmly. 'Why don't we all go and watch it?'

'Great idea!' Brett enthused, looking at Magnus and Catriona. 'What do you say?'

Magnus was looking pale, Fiona flushed and excited, and it was on the tip of Catriona's tongue to suggest that they went alone when Magnus said harshly:

'Why not? It'll be a change to get off this damned island.'

Catriona stared at him, puzzled by his changed mood.

'I didn't realise you and Magnus had attended an Up-Helly-Aa together,' she murmured to Fiona curiously later. 'He never told me.'

'Perhaps he didn't think it important enough,' Fiona replied lightly. She had gone quite pale and although she smiled Catriona saw the deep pain at the back of her eyes, as they rested on Magnus.

He had behaved churlishly towards Fiona ever since she arrived, Catriona realised suddenly. She would have to speak to him about it. Fiona was an old and good friend, even though she did appear to be finding more pleasure in Brett's company than theirs. The two of them were swapping stories of life in the more inaccessible parts of the world. Fiona had done a year's voluntary work before taking up her present job at a large Edinburgh hospital.

'You were in South America, weren't you, Magnus?' she queried suddenly, turning towards him. 'When you were with United Oil.'

'If you'll all excuse me, I think I'll go up to bed,' Magnus announced, ignoring the question. His face was white, whether with anger or pain Catriona could not tell, and looking at Fiona she wondered whether the other girl's question had been deliberate or an accident.

'I think I'll go too,' she said when Magnus had gone.

Mac was poring over a medical journal, and neither Brett nor Fiona showed any signs of wanting to move.

'Is there any chance of getting out to one of the

rigs this time, Mac?' Fiona asked her uncle as Catriona opened the door. 'I'm fascinated by them.'

'They're dry and womanless,' Mac said wryly, 'and both rules are rigorously enforced, with good reason. Those men are doing a very dangerous job and can't afford to take chances. We had a laddie last week nearly lost his leg, and all for a moment's carelessness. Cut right through a vein and the blood was shooting up like a gusher.'

'If you're really keen I think it could be arranged,' Brett cut in quietly. 'I could have a word with a friend of mine.'

'Oh, would you?' Fiona enthused excitedly. She was not strictly a pretty girl, but her pert features possessed an animation and sparkle that made Catriona feel drab in comparison.

'I'll see what I can do,' Brett promised with an indulgent smile—a smile such as he had never given her, Catriona thought bitterly. He looked up, catching her off guard, his eyes resting perceptively on her as she deliberately made her face blank.

'What about you, Catriona? Will you be joining us?'

'Of course she will,' Fiona said gaily before Catriona could speak. 'And Magnus too. It will do him good. And now how about changing that dressing of yours?' she said, standing up and waiting for Brett to catch up with her. It was only natural that she should take on this task—after all, she was a trained nurse—but Catriona could not contain the shaft of bitter jealousy stabbing through her as she thought about the two of them together in the intimacy of Brett's bedroom. Would he goad Fiona in the same way as he had done her? Hardly. Fiona had made no secret of the fact that she found him attractive. Sexy, she had called him, and he was, Catriona admitted, with a subtle, powerful sensuality that undermined all her own carefully nurtured defences so that his mere touch was enough to make her entire body ache for his possession.

Over breakfast Brett told them that he had arranged for them to visit the rig on Boxing Day.

'The chopper will pick us up and bring us back.'

Catriona had half expected Magnus to refuse to go, but since Brett appeared to take it for granted that he would be going, she suspected that her brother had no wish to appear churlish by backing out. By the same token she felt compelled to accept as well, although for different reasons. She had no wish for Brett to guess exactly why she could not bear to see him and Fiona together, his dark head bent protectively over her golden one, as it was now. Fiona had been asking about the rig, and he had drawn her a small diagram. He was still not able to dive and since Mac had suggested that a brisk walk would not come amiss, Catriona was left alone in the house with him while the others took an ecstatic Russet out on to the hill.

The small sketch was lying on the table when she started to clear away the dishes. Almost involuntarily her fingers closed round it, trembling slightly as they came in contact with the paper. A movement by the door betrayed Brett's presence and she dropped the paper as though it were alive.

'I didn't know you were interested in engineering.' He bent to retrieve the drawing as it fluttered to the floor, and all the love she felt for him welled up in an uncontrollable wave as she looked down at his dark head.

He straightened abruptly and she could only stare

wordlessly at him, mesmerised by the faint shadowing of dark chest hair where his shirt was unfastened.
Her fingers curled tightly into her palms and she
wondered if he actually thought Fiona had a genuine
interest in engineering, or if he had guessed that her
interest lay more with him.

He was proffering the sketch and she ignored his
outstretched hand.

'I'm not,' she told him coldly. 'I just wondered
what it was.'

She thought she heard him sigh, resignation in the
hand which dropped to his side after screwing up
the paper into a small ball and tossing it on the fire.

She leaned forward, to reach past him for the salt
and pepper, and almost overbalanced, his hands
steadying when she would have fallen. She thanked
him coolly, not daring to look up into his face, and
tried to move away. His hands still gripped her
arms.

'What's going on between Fiona and Magnus?'
he asked suddenly. 'Oh, come on, you can't be that
blind?' he demanded incredulously, looking down
into her startled face. 'You could have cut the atmosphere between the two of them with a knife last
night. What's happening? Or is it already over?'

Her heart dropped with a sickening jolt. He would
make a heaven on earth for the woman he loved,
Fiona had said, and Brett was making no secret of
the fact that he was very interested in Fiona, even to
the extent of making sure that she wasn't involved
with anyone else.

'Why don't you ask Fiona that yourself?' she
demanded. 'I'm sure you're on intimate enough
terms with her.' She tried to shrug him aside as she
spoke, but he was too strong for her and the next

moment his mouth was depriving her of breath as it locked on hers in furious punishment, the pressure of his arms forcing her against him until she was aware of every hard muscle.

His kiss sapped her of the will to resist, insistently demanding her surrender to its potency. Her lips parted on a soft moan, her hands crushed against the warmth of Brett's chest.

When he released her Brett was still breathing hard, his eyes glittering with a narrowed watchfulness that sent her pulses racing.

'At last I've managed to find a way of silencing that vituperative tongue,' he mocked derisively. 'Perhaps I ought to patent it.'

'And perhaps I ought to tell Fiona exactly what kind of man you are!' Catriona challenged, close to tears. But she knew she wouldn't, and when the others came back, if any of them noticed that she was oddly silent they made no mention of it.

Findlay arrived during the afternoon with the Christmas tree he had brought from Lerwick. Real Christmas trees were a luxury in the Shetlands, and Catriona's eyes stung slightly as she and Fiona dressed it. The last time they had had a real tree had been the Christmas before her parents were drowned; and that Christmas had stayed in her mind as all that Christmas should really be. There was no church on Falla, but that had not stopped them holding their own special service attended by all the crofters.

'I mind fine the last time I saw a Christmas tree in this house,' Findlay commented softly, following her train of thought. They had persuaded him to have a 'wee dram' and he had been entertaining them with fishing stories he had heard at his grand-father's knee.

'Will you be going back to London?' Fiona asked as they attached the dainty coloured lights.

'When Magnus is better. He did so much for me that I want to repay him in full now that I can.'

'Have you thought that he might recover a lot faster if he were left to his own devices?' Fiona asked lightly. 'You're making it too easy for him to hide from the rest of the world, Cat.'

Was that a kind way of telling her that she was smothering Magnus? She looked covertly at Fiona, watching the efficient, economical movements of the other girl's capable hands, and then glancing across at her brother. For a moment his unguarded expression as he watched Fiona held all the longing and bitterness she herself experienced when she looked at Brett, and it came to her with shocked comprehension that Magnus was in love with Fiona.

He looked across, as though sensing her regard, his face close and shuttered, and she knew with a feeling of sadness that he would not confide his feelings to her, just as she could not confide hers to him.

With Fiona's assistance she spent the rest of the day baking mince pies, and when Findlay finally announced that he was leaving the kitchen was fragrant with the smell of their cooking. As he reached the door he felt in his jacket pocket and grinning sheepishly produced a small sprig of mistletoe.

Catriona laughed and kissed his leathery cheek, making him redden faintly.

'Away wi' ye, lassie,' he protested, 'Save that for yon young man.'

Catriona hadn't seen Brett walk in, and she deliberately handed the mistletoe to her brother.

'I think you'll have more use for this than me, Magnus,' she told him lightly, but although Fiona was sitting temptingly on the edge of the kitchen table, well within kissing range, he simply ignored the invitation and shrugged on an old anorak, announcing that he was going out.

'Looks like that just leaves you and me,' Brett commented to Fiona, pinning the offending piece of greenery on to one of the kitchen beams and kissing Fiona lingering on the mouth.

Catriona forced herself not to leave the room. Her body felt as though it were being ripped apart. To prevent herself from crying out aloud she went to the oven and opened the door. In her anxiety not to witness the embrace she moved clumsily, burning her hand on the door, her involuntary gasp of pain drawing a concerned exclamation from Fiona, who hurried over to inspect the reddening flesh.

'Nasty,' she commented briefly. 'I've got some stuff upstairs, I'll run and get it.'

When Catriona was alone with Brett her eyes went involuntarily to the mistletoe hanging from the rafter.

'Don't worry, you're quite safe,' he told her sardonically.

Of course she was! He wasn't likely to kiss her when he could kiss Fiona!

'This will take the heat out of it,' Fiona promised, re-entering the kitchen. 'I'll just smear a bit on. Mmm, you're getting a lovely blister.' She turned to the oven and deftly removed the mince pies, taking them through to the larder, where her approving surprise was perfectly audible.

'When did you get the freezer?' she exclaimed.

'Brett bought it for . . . for the men,' Catriona told

her curtly. 'They need proper meat meals every day, and we can't guarantee that on Falla without.'

'Well, I think it was very thoughtful of him,' Fiona announced firmly, smiling at Brett. 'And it's certainly a good deal more than Magnus has ever thought to do.'

'And it's very pleasant to be appreciated,' Brett drawled, returning her smile.

There was a huge lump in Catriona's throat and she knew she had to escape before she disgraced herself completely.

'Excuse me,' she began bitterly. 'I don't want to spoil your mutual admiration society!'

'Oh dear, do you think we've upset her?' she heard Fiona asking in concern as she fled, but Brett's response, whatever it was, was lost in the banging of the kitchen door.

It was plain that Magnus shared her reluctance to visit the rig, Catriona thought, watching her brother huddled up against the door of the helicopter, his expression withdrawn as he stared down at the wind-tossed seas.

From up here Falla was a small green splodge set in the unending grey backcloth which stretched from horizon to horizon.

'Ever been up in one of these things before?' the young American pilot asked Catriona with a grin. His low whistle of appreciation as he had helped her into the helicopter had made her blush faintly, uncomfortably aware of Brett's sardonic presence. He was wearing close-fitting jeans, and a thick woollen sweater beneath his casual leather jacket; almost a uniform up here in the Shetlands, but on him somehow much more disturbingly masculine. No wonder Fiona was sticking so determinedly to his side, she thought, admonishing herself for the bitchiness her jealousy had provoked.

Until she had met Brett Simons she had thought herself a very level-headed female; apart from the odd teenage crush there had been no man to set her pulses racing and when she had thought about marriage—which had been very infrequently—it had been with some vague idea of marrying a man with whom she had shared interests and felt completely comfortable.

Comfortable was the last word anyone in their right mind would apply to Brett, and yet she knew that once she had met him there could never be any other man with whom she could share the intimacies of marriage. Her body, previously so well-behaved and controllable, seemed to have developed a will of its own, a will which grew stronger by the day, so that every time she looked at Brett she was struck by some new sensual aspect of his appearance she had not previously noticed. Like the sure knowledge of her sex she now sensed in him; the male strength, mated with devastating tenderness. Brett was a man who respected women as well as desiring them; at least, all other women. He had shown a demoralising lack of either emotion so far as she was concerned.

'There she blows,' Mac commented jocularly as the rig hove into view.

'It's an it, not a she, Mac,' Fiona reproved, wrinkling her nose. 'Did you know that the Shetlanders were once whalers?' she asked Brett. 'Long before whaling became so commercialised.'

'Don't!' Catriona begged, shuddering. She knew it was ridiculous, but the plight of those magnificent, peaceful mammals reached out to her, and she could not bear to think of their savage decimation.

'Compassion? You do surprise me,' Brett commented in a hard voice.

The pilot drew their attention to the approaching rig and observing the tiny landing space Catriona felt faintly sick.

'You'd think we'd get a whole heap of snow up hereabouts, being so far north,' he commented as he manoeuvred the helicopter expertly earthwards. 'I'd just love to write home to Florida and tell my folks that I've seen real live snow.'

Catriona laughed.

'I'm afraid you're not likely to. You've got the Gulf Stream to thank for you, it keeps the temperature pretty even all year round, although of course it is warmer in the summer and we do get the long hours of daylight.'

'You can say that again! I'd never seen the sun set at mightnight until I came up here. Sure was a sight worth seeing.'

'White nights,' Catriona told him knowledgeably, 'that's what the Russian aristocracy used to call them. Whenever I'm away from the islands, it's the skies I miss the most; the continuously changing pattern of the clouds—that, and the sea.'

Brett was looking at her curiously, and she blushed furiously with herself for being caught out in such a foolish flight of fancy.

'That's odd,' Brett commented in a soft, deep voice. 'It's the skies up here that I find so endlessly fascinating, among other things.' He and Fiona exchanged a smile and white-hot jealousy knifed through Catriona. Was Fiona one of the things he found fascinating? They certainly seemed to have grown very close in a remarkably short span of time. She glanced at Magnus. He was staring out of the window, his knuckles white against his clenched flesh. They made a good pair, she thought savagely, both of them languishing after a love that could never be theirs.

Brett's friend made them extremely welcome. He had flown out to the rig from Sullom Voe especially to show them round, diplomatically ignoring the grinning appreciation of the watching roustabouts and roughnecks as he produced helmets for Catriona and Fiona.

'Sorry about the lack of glamour,' he apologised with a smile. 'But we make it a rule on the rigs that all personnel must wear helmets.'

'Very wise too,' Fiona approved firmly.

Was it by accident or design that she and Brett had walked forward together, Brett's hand protectively cupping her elbow, while she was forced to fall back with Mac and Magnus?

Chris made their tour very interesting, and before long Magnus was questioning him closely on several points of marine engineering, his features a good deal more animated than they had been when they had stepped on to the rig platform.

'Come down to the office and I'll get you all a cup of tea,' Chris offered when the tour was over. 'Sorry it can't be anything stronger, but rules are rules, and we can't expect the men to keep them if we blatantly break them ourselves.'

The tea was sweet and strong, from the cafeteria on the rig.

'Completely staffed by men,' Chris told them. 'That's another rule we're pretty keen on—no women. Although we do occasionally make the odd exception.'

When they went back up to the platform for the

return journey Brett leaned out over the superstructure to examine it more closely. Catriona watched him with her heart in her mouth, terrified that he might fall. They were several hundred feet above sea level and any man falling into those turbulent seas from such a height could have little chance of surviving.

Almost as though her thought were father to the deed, Catriona gasped in horror as Brett suddenly leaned out too far, and overbalanced.

Her terrified cry was caught by the wind, Magnus turning instinctively at the sound and realising instantly what had happened. Before anyone could stop him he was pulling off his jacket, following Brett into the angry seas, with a knife-clean dive.

'Someone throw them a lifebelt!' Chris snapped out curtly.

Catriona was dragged back from the edge of the rig by Mac's protective arm as ordered chaos broke out all around them.

'Could . . . could you see them?' she begged Mac, in a voice that trembled. 'Were . . .'

'Dinna fret, lassie,' Mac urged her, his Scots accent broadening with anxiety. 'If anone can save yon laddie it will be Magnus. A powerful fine swimmer he was as a laddie.'

A small motorboat had been launched and the sound of its engine sawed through the afternoon. The roustabouts were gathered on the edge of the rig, scanning the waves anxiously.

'I see one!' Catriona heard one call, while her heart lurched in agony. One—either her brother or the man she loved; either way she lost.

'Aye, and there's yon other,' a broad Scots voice proclaimed excitedly.

'Mac . . .'

'Wait here,' he told her tersely. 'I'll find out what's happening.'

He was back two minutes later, beaming with relief.

'Young Magnus has done a fine job. The boat will be picking them up any moment now. Neatest dive I've seen in a long time. He must have hit the water only seconds after Brett. He's a brave laddie. There's not many who would have acted so quickly, nor so courageously.'

And so needlessly, Catriona thought numbly. Because she had seen Brett quite deliberately let go of the steel girder. Quite, quite deliberately.

Within half an hour both men were back on the rig, wrapped in dry towels in Chris's office, and drinking steaming mugs of tea, while Mac pronounced them both perfectly healthy.

'Heads like rubber,' he announced with a beam. 'And just as well!'

'They should both be in bed,' Fiona interrupted briskly, suddenly very much the nurse. 'Especially Magnus. His pulse is racing.'

Hardly surprising, Catriona thought dryly, seeing that Fiona was easily within kissing distance, her competent fingers clasped round his wrist.

'Umm, and they ought to have X-rays,' Mac added.

'I'll have the 'copter take you to Lerwick,' Chris offered, and so Catriona found herself alone in the house, with only the Christmas tree for company, while Mac and Fiona attended to their patients in Lerwick.

She was sitting in a high-backed leather chair in front of the fire, her mind going over and over the events of the afternoon like a film run backwards in slow motion, always stopping at that fatal moment when Brett had quite deliberately let go of the girder. But why?

The phone rang and she shifted in her chair, reaching for it. As she suspected it was Mac calling to tell her that the hospital were keeping Magnus in overnight.

'Slight shock, nothing to worry about,' he reassured her. 'And probably more psychological than physical. That was a very brave thing he did this afternoon, Cat, especially for a man who thinks his nerve's completely gone. See you soon.'

He rang off before she could question him further. She was curled up in the chair, warm and sleepy, with no incitement to go upstairs and get undressed.

Magnus had bought her a new housecoat for Christmas; it was pure silk, a soft mauve blue which deepened her eyes, the revers and edges all bound in silver-grey satin. He had ordered it from an exlusive London store and she had chided him for the extravagance even while appreciating it.

There had been small gifts from Mac and Fiona and she in return had got Mac some special waterproof knitted socks knitted by Shetland women, something which she knew he would welcome, and an expensive bottle of scent for Fiona.

Brett's addition to the house-party had worried her. She could think of no small impersonal gift suitable for him, and common sense and lack of resources precluded her from making the sort of madly extravagant gesture her heart urged. In the end she had contented herself with some cologne she had bought for Magnus, receiving in turn some equally impersonal handmade chocolates.

It hadn't been one of her happiest Christmases on

record, she thought wryly; watching Brett's dark head constantly close to Fiona's fair one had seen to that.

There was something about the feel of silk next to one's skin, she reflected, moving sensuously, her breasts peaking beneath the moulding fabric. Since Brett's intrusion into her life she had be more aware of her body as never before—and its needs.

She was on the verge of sleep when the library door opened, the sudden shaft of cold air startling her almost out of her skin.

'Mac?' she called hesitantly, hating herself for the tremor of fear in her voice. What was she frightened of? The ghost of the long-dead Peterson who had built this house?

' 'Fraid not.' Brett's voice came sardonically from the shadows, as he reached for the light switch, flooding the room with light.

Blinking disbelievingly, Catriona stared up at him.

'What are you doing here?' His face seemed faintly flushed, a glaze in his eyes which made hers narrow in swift comprehension. Had Brett been drinking?

'Couldn't leave you here all alone, so we drew straws.'

'And you were unlucky? You should have asked Mac to swop with you. He wouldn't have minded.'

'He needed his sleep, and besides, there was something I wanted to talk to you about.'

'Like why you deliberately faked that fall? Why did you do it? Or did it just seem like a good idea at the time? A rather hit-and-miss way of getting rid of a rival,' she sneered bitterly.

'I've had just about as much of this as I can stand.' White grooves of bitter anger were carved either side of his mouth, his eyes almost black as they surveyed her with cold contempt. 'Is that what you honestly think? That I fell off that rig just to try and get rid of Magnus?'

She was beginning to feel slightly ashamed of the accusation. Put like that, in Brett's sardonic voice, it did sound faintly ridiculous.

'Then why did you do it?' she demanded, sitting upright in her chair. The jerky movement tautened the fine silk fabric across her breasts, and Brett followed it for a second before letting his eyes linger thoughtfully along the length of her body.

'Are you wearing anything under that thing?' he asked in a voice which made it clear that he already knew the answer. 'What a strange female you are, to be sure! All the ones I know only dress like that when they're expecting company, not when they know they're going to be alone. Are you frightened of your sexuality, Catriona? Is that why you hide it away behind those jeans and sweaters?'

'Jeans and sweaters are the only suitable outdoor wear for the Shetlands,' she told him briskly, hoping he hadn't noticed the sudden betraying flush on her cheeks. 'You were telling me about your "accident",' she reminded him.

'Ah yes.' He eyed her thoughtfully for a second. 'It first occurred to me the other day when we were out diving. Despite his contention that he isn't fit to go back to his old job Magnus was prepared to dive into the voe if necessary to save my life. What would happen, I wondered, if he was faced with a real emergency? I felt sure that if that emergency could be created it would break through his barriers, overcome his trauma. You see, his fear stemmed from the fact that before, during his accident he hadn't been able to help his friends, had been unable to move, but I was sure that in different circumstances, given the ability to move frequently he would find that his courage hadn't deserted him at all, that it was simply in hiding.'

'Quite the amateur psychologist, aren't we?' Catriona interrupted tightly. 'And so you set it all up, did you? Priming your friend Chris and all his staff to stand by just in case your little ploy didn't work? Didn't it occur to you that my brother could have been killed, that . . .'

'Just a moment . . .' His hands grasped her flailing fists, pinioning them firmly as he stood over her, and despite everything her traitorous heart still missed a beat at his proximity.

'No one had any inkling of what I intended, apart from me. And as for Magnus—well, I already knew he was a first class diver and swimmer.'

'But to take such a risk . . .' She was weakening and she knew it. 'You could have been killed—both of you!'

Brett grimaced slightly.

'No way. I merely took a chance that beneath his fear Magnus still had his training, his instinct, which in a moment of pure necessity would overcome everything else. We talked in the hospital, and I think he's over the worst. I've told him if he wants it he can always have a job with me . . .'

Tears pricked her eyes.

'Still hating me?' he demanded roughly. 'Resenting me because you weren't the one to free him from his trauma? Oh yes, Mac told me how desperately you wanted to.'

The tears welled and fell.

'Is that how you see me?' she asked brokenly. 'The

sort of jealous, bigoted person who would feel like
that? Do you think I care who freed Magnus as long
as it was achieved?'

He smiled wryly at her fierceness.

'So I was wrong. It seems to be a fault of mine
these days.'

He released her wrists and walked towards the
door, snapping off the light.

'Sweet dreams, Catriona.'

His hand was on the door handle when his sharp
ears caught the sound of her first muffled sob. He
paused, his shadow still as though still not sure that
he had interpreted the small sound correctly, and
then as his eyes pierced the darkness, the shudders
which racked her slight body, her sobs stifled by the
hand pressed tight against her mouth, brought him
instantly to her side, her arms placed gently round
his neck so that he could lift her and draw her down
against him, stroking back the tumbled curls from
her forehead while he comforted her with soothing
words.

'That's right, cry it out,' he urged her softly. 'It's
just shock. Don't bottle it up; let it all out . . .'

CHAPTER EIGHT

ONLY it wasn't shock that was making her body
tremble against him, Catriona thought hazily
moments later when the storm of weeping was over;
and neither was the comfort she sought from him
avuncular. Brett might be treating her very much as
though she were a small, frightened child, but that

was not how her body was reacting to his. She could smell the male tang of his body, acutely conscious of the warm flesh and smooth muscles concealed by his clothes. Her need of him overcame every other emotion, her hands clinging feverishly to him as he bent down to free them. As though it were happening in slow motion she saw his expression change, her body taking fire from the desire suddenly burning in the jade eyes. This time she wasn't going to dissect or question; she was simply going to seize the moment. Today he could have been killed, and the knowledge of how it had felt to fear that they no longer shared the same world would be with her for ever.

She met his kiss with blind yearning, her mouth parting with an abandon she had never visualised, her fingers tugging impatiently at the thick sweater, imparting her need for a closer contact with the male flesh so enticingly close to her own.

For a moment Brett held her off, his eyes searching her passion-filled features, and then with a muttered, 'Any man who refuses the gods when they offer him this is a fool,' his arms closed round her in fierce demand, his mouth parting hers in a kiss that stripped away everything but the need to assuage the ache slowly building up inside her.

And yet his hands on her body were still gentle, as though he knew her inexperience and was holding himself in check because of it. But that wasn't what Catrina wanted. If she was to have only this one memory of him, let them at least meet as equals, and her body communicated this to him, urging him to passionate possession of the flesh he was revealing to the firelight glow.

His hands on her breasts were reverent, the

warmth of his mouth against her throat sending dizzying waves of pleasure through her. She moaned in protest as the warmth was removed, only to gasp in delirium as his lips moved gently against the gilded peaks of her breasts.

The aching yearning became a frenzied need, her hands sliding up beneath his sweater to clench pleadingly against the muscles of his back while she looked down at the dark head against her breast with all her love revealed in her eyes.

'Catriona, look at me.'

As the dark head lifted, she obeyed the rough command, shyness suddenly overcoming her as the firelight showed her his very real desire. As he drew away from her she shivered convulsively, pulsating with a deep longing for closer union.

'Don't stop, Brett,' she moaned feverishly, clutching his arm. 'Don't stop touching me!'

His breath rasped against her skin as he caught her up in his arms, removing the silk barrier before studying every inch of her body with a look that made her moan faintly with desire.

'Let me look at you, Brett,' she begged hoarsely. 'Let me look at you.'

He removed his clothes in silence, his eyes never leaving her face. Her pulses raced frantically, her mouth dry with an unbearable tension.

'You're beautiful,' she said slowly, awed by the discovery, her fingertips touching him delicately. He trembled suddenly, her head falling back against his supporting arm as his lips returned to her now tautly erect breasts. This time he wasn't gentle, and she didn't want him to be, her breath coming in sobbing rasps as she arched imploringly against him, his laboured breathing intensely exciting as he pulled her tightly against him. His mouth left fire where it touched, prompting her own lips to make sensual forays along his flesh. His sudden muttered, 'Catriona,' held an urgency that melted the flesh from her bones, her longing to know his full possession so intense that it overwhelmed everything else. She had deliberately blotted out the fact that he didn't love her, telling herself that she would be grateful for the crumbs of his passion, but as the heated thrashing movements of her body increased she sensed his sudden tension and withdrawal, and although her fingers fluttered pleadingly against the taut flatness of his stomach their message was ignored. Her hands were grasped firmly, and she was held ignominiously away from him while he looked at her through the darkness.

'Oh no . . .' he began softly. 'Not this time. You go to my head like . . .'

The phone started to ring and she reached for it automatically. It was Fiona, sounding surprised that she had answered and asking for Brett. As she passed the receiver over, somehow she found the courage to say brittly:

'Don't worry about it. I'll save you the embarrassment of being the one to say it. I appeal to your baser instincts and you're very sorry that it happened and will I please not tell Fiona.' Tears had started to roll down her cheeks, but she turned away so that he would not see them. 'My God, do you think I'm proud of it?' She thrust the receiver into his hands and somehow managed to stumble out of the room, shaking with a mixture of shame and—much as she hated to admit it—deprivation.

How could she have been so stupid! Another few minutes and Brett would have seen how she felt. She

would not have been able to hide it from him. And
the shame of having him restrain her. She almost
felt physically sick with rejection. It was different for
men—they could make love when only experiencing
desire, but Brett had a tender conscience, a compassionate regard for other people's feelings. Witness his
desire to help Magnus, and his unwillingness to hurt
Fiona by making love to her, even while willing to
admit to her his aroused desire. Her foolish dreams
had turned to dust.

Although she lay sleepless long into the night she
never heard him come to bed. If only there was some
way of suddenly transporting herself several thousands of miles away where she need never set eyes
on him again, and yet at the same time she knew
that being deprived of the ability to do so would be
like being deprived of air.

If she hadn't seen it with her own eyes, she would
not have been able to believe the change in Magnus.
Gone was the introverted stranger who had come
back from the Middle East and in his place was the
elder brother she had always adored. His gaunt
frame had started to fill out again and he and Brett
spent hours poring over blueprints and scale draw-
ings of the proposed terminal.

The gale which had blown up following Magnus's
return to Falla with Fiona kept them all indoors.
Mac had stayed in Lerwick, prevented from returning by a shortage of staff at the hospital, and watching Magnus, Brett and Fiona laughing together over
the Monopoly board she felt a searing shaft of pain.

The morning before Magnus's return to Falla
she had not known how she was going to face Brett.

He was already in the kitchen when she got
downstairs, the dark shadow along his jaw evidence

that he had still to shave and somehow disturbingly reminiscent of all that happened the night before.

He had looked so carelessly handsome, so competently in control that her courage had almost deserted her, but she knew that if she did not face him now she would never be able to do so.

He was wearing a brief towelling robe, his legs bare beneath the hem, covered in fine dark hairs, and her eyes were drawn against her will along the potently masculine length of his body.

'Tea?' he asked mundanely, lifting the brown earthenware teapot from the oven.

Catriona nodded her head, her heart aching over the mock-domesticity. Anyone watching them now would think them a comfortably married couple sharing an early morning cup of tea before facing the day.

'Sugar?' She shook her head, pushing the blonde hair back in a gesture which was vaguely defensive.

'We've got to talk.'

The abrupt announcement stilled the hand she had reached out for her tea.

'Talk?' Her mouth was dry, and she touched her lips lightly with her tongue, flushing as Brett's eyes narrowed over the unconsciously provocative movement. 'What about?'

'About last night,' Brett replied unequivocally, 'I know that what happened was as a result of the emotional impact of the accident . . .'

'And a complete mistake,' Catriona interrupted in an unsteady voice. 'So let's just forget it, shall we?'

'If that's what you want.' His voice sounded like iron, and she could not bear to look at him. Bending her face over the mug she was clasping with both hands, she replied as calmly as she could, horribly aware of the unnaturally high tone of her voice.

'It is.'

Despite the warmth of the kitchen she was feeling terribly cold, colder than she had ever felt in her life, and that included the day they had brought the news of her parents' death. What she was experiencing was like death in a way, only a thousand times more painful because this pain, the pain of denying her emotions, would live within her for always.

'Very well.'

Brett's mug was placed carefully on the table, his expression as he glanced at her just once totally impersonal, and that was the way it had been ever since.

Suppressing a sigh, she watched him smiling at Fiona, his eyes alight with laughter, and then as though he was conscious of her watching him he looked across at her, the laughter dying out of his face to be replaced by cold civility. He was looking through her, not at her, she acknowledged miserably.

'Why don't you come and join in?' Magnus urged her. 'You used to love Monopoly.'

'Maybe she still does, but she isn't too keen on the company,' Brett offered sardonically. He had taken to making these bitingly succinct comments, in fact his whole attitude towards her had changed since that fateful night. Perhaps now that he and Magnus were on such excellent terms he no longer cared what opinion she had of him. The way in which he had removed her hands from his body would stay with her as long as she lived. Just to think of it made her tremble with shame. Was that why he was now so cold? Was he frightened that she might have read too much into his merely sexual desire?

The extremely bad gales they were suffering kept them housebound. Fiona had been as good as her word concerning the household chores and Catriona found herself with more time on her hands than she had known for many months.

'What are you going to do with yourself, Cat?' Magnus asked her one afternoon when they were alone together in the library. 'Now that I know that my fears about my ability to work were groundless I think I ought to look around me for a new job. Brett has offered me one with him—with the possibility of a partnership, but of course that all hinges on what happens with the terminal.'

'You mean unless we agree to it there won't be any job?' she enquired contemptuously. 'You don't need Brett Simons' charity, Magnus. You could get your old job back with United Oil.'

'You're jumping to conclusions—and silly ones at that. No, Brett's offer doesn't hinge on our agreement to the terminal, but whether I can afford to take up his offer of partnership must, otherwise where would I find the money to go in with him—and besides, although from the sound of it his business is doing very well, the construction of the terminal is bound to have impressive effect upon it.'

'He's got it all planned out, hasn't he? Honestly, Magnus, I don't know how you can contemplate working with him. Or don't you care that he's stolen Fiona from under your nose?'

She realised the moment she saw her brother's face that she had gone too far. It was grim and determined.

'Fiona was never mine to steal, let's get that clearly understood, Cat. And if she prefers Brett to me—well, I haven't exactly been ideal marriage material recently, have I? Going in with Brett will give me the chance to take a broader view; there is a limit to how long a man can remain a field geologist, you know, Cat. But we weren't talking about me, we were discussing you, and your plans. Will you go back to London and continue with your course?'

'I don't suppose I've got much option. I can't expect you to support me for the rest of my life.'

'If the terminal goes ahead you'll probably be able to support yourself quite adequately without ever lifting a finger again,' Magnus told her quietly. 'Cat, what's wrong? I know I've been a selfish brute recently, but I can't help thinking that all is not as it should be. Is it Brett?'

Her head shot up.

'I don't like him, if that's what you mean,' she agreed defiantly. 'Oh, I know he's helped you tremendously, and for that I'm grateful, but he's exacted payment for it, hasn't he? First the terminal, and now Fiona?'

'Oh, Cat,' Magnus said, so gently that for some reason she felt tears pricking her eyes. 'You don't fool me, my dear. I know you too well. You're in love with him, aren't you?'

'Is it so very obvious?'

'Only to me,' he assured her. 'Look, love, I'm not trying to get rid of you, but I think it's time you started thinking about your future. Staying here brooding won't do any good . . .'

'And besides, if the terminal goes ahead Brett will be here, and we don't want me embarrassing him with my unrequited love, do we?'

'Oh, Cat!' His voice was exasperated. 'That wasn't

what I meant at all. I was simply thinking of you. Stay if you like . . .'

'And watch him with Fiona?'

Magnus blenched and she was instantly remorseful. Perhaps Magnus was right and it would be for the best if she left as soon as possible. There was now little doubt in her mind that the terminal would go ahead. From the snatches of conversation she had overheard between Brett and Magnus it was plain that the voe had more than fulfilled its potential, and she knew that when the time came it would be impossible for her to refuse her consent. Brett had everything organised, she thought unhappily, and Fiona would make him an excellent wife.

She went to bed early, refusing the others' invitation to join them by the fire. How on earth Magnus could remain so apparently unperturbed she did not know, but then her brother seemed to be labouring under the unselfish wish that Fiona might find the happiness he thought she deserved and so was content to accept her growing intimacy with Brett, whereas she could not even look at them without being pierced by the most acute jealousy.

She awoke to a clear sky, the wind had dropped, but she knew better than to imagine that the respite was anything other than temporary. Skipping breakfast, she went down to the harbour and watched Findlay prepare his fishing yaol.

'Going out?' She was sitting on the harbour wall, her knees drawn up under her chin, her hair in one single plait.

'Aye, although I doubt not the wind will be back before nightfall.'

'Can I come with you?'

He watched the restless plucking motion of her

fingers, saw the pain shadowing her eyes and the pallor of her skin.

'Verra well, but I'll have no slacking, mind.'

The fishy-tarry smell of the old yaol took Catriona back instantly to her childhood. How often had she and Magnus sneaked out of the house at dawn on summer mornings to go out with the fishing boats? Falla's fleet was much smaller now, most of the younger men working for the larger companies based in Lerwick, but one or two, like Findlay, still fished these waters.

The sea was choppy and she sat in silence as Findlay manoeuvred the small boat out of the harbour, moving instinctively to work at his side as he started to lay the lobster pots.

'I doubt they'll bring in much, but you never know.'

'Pessimist!' she teased. Findlay kept looking up at the sky as they worked, and as he had predicted, before too long ominous black clouds masked the horizon.

'Time to move. That's a north-easter gathering up there, unless I'm much mistaken.'

They were within sight of Falla when Catriona spotted the small dinghy. It was tacking briskly before the wind, the red and yellow sails a gay banner against the grey sea. She drew Findlay's attention to the small craft.

'Aren't those the Lerwick Sailing Club's colours?'

'Aye,' he agreed grimly. 'Some bluidy fool seeing a patch of blue sky and thinking summer's come. An incomer, I'll mak' na doubt. The wind will be up before he's within five miles of Lerwick.' He picked up the hailer lying at the bottom of the yaol and bellowed to the solitary yachtsman to come alongside

The yachtsman was wearing a bright orange inflatable jacket, his fair hair nearly as light as Catriona's in the sun. He heard Findlay's voice and waved cheerfully to them, the fragile dinghy heading straight for the dangerous saw-toothed rocks concealed by the high tide.

'Yon bitty craft will be smashed up like pulp against the Needles,' Findlay prophesied in disgust. 'Feckless fool!'

'Findlay, we must do something. He'll be carried away by the current if the dinghy turns over, you know how strong it is there.'

'Like a millrace,' Findlay agreed gloomily, shouting a warning across the waves.

Either the yachtsman had not heard it, or he thought they were exaggerating, for with another wave he tacked again, setting the dinghy straight for the concealed rocks.

Findlay muttered something highly uncomplimentary under his breath and started to follow him, the old yaol wallowing in the fierce currents as he tried to make speed.

A sudden gust of wind caught the red and yellow sail, and as Catriona watched the dingy keeled over and was caught in the racing current and swept furiously towards the Needles.

Her heart in her mouth, she watched as the sailor kicked free of the doomed dinghy, trying to swim against the fast current.

'Throw him a line,' Findlay instructed curtly, 'and I'll try and get closer in to him. Won't do any good if we all end up being swept to our deaths!'

Findlay took them as close to the current as was possible, the lifebelt Catriona had flung into the turbulent waters sweeping swiftly down towards the endangered man. For a moment she thought he had missed it, and was all ready to throw the second, when Findlay said dryly, 'Bide, lassie, he's caught hold.'

When they pulled him on board he was out of breath and soaked through. Findlay turned the yaol's nose towards Falla, giving their unexpected passenger one grimly contemptuous glance as he shook his head rather like a dog emerging from water and exclaimed cheerfully, 'That was lucky! Fierce currents you have round here.'

'Aye, and like as not your body would have been washed up on one of our beaches had we not been here. Visitor, are you?'

'Is it that obvious?' he asked, grinning at Catriona. He seemed none the worse for his experience, and now that the fair hair plastered drippingly to his skull was beginning to dry, she saw that he was extremely attractive. Lightweight, but fun, she decided, listening to his explanation of how he had been staying with his brother in Lerwick, and how he had decided to take the dinghy out while his brother and sister-in-law were out.

The wind had returned and Catriona knew that Findlay had been right to forecast more gales for the evening.

'I'm afraid we can't take you back to Lerwick,' she apologised as their companion introduced himself as Tim Fielding.

'Oh, don't worry about it. Alan, my brother, will probably send a chopper over for me.' He spoke with the careless assurance of the very wealthy.

Findlay glowered at him from under his eyebrows. 'Like as not nothing will be able to put down on Falla in this wind,' was his only comment.

'Not exactly friendly, is he?' Tim murmured in an aside to Catriona. 'Mmm, wait until they here about this back in London!' He had seen her properly for the first time and his eyes were frankly appreciative. 'You're not a mermaid by any chance, are you?' He glanced down at her workmanlike jeans and waders and grinned disarmingly. 'No, definitely no trace of a tail there.'

'You shouldn't have been sailing alone in these waters,' Catriona told him severely. 'You realise if we hadn't been here that you would probably have drowned? The currents round here are notorious.'

'I'll know better next time, ma'am,' he agreed mock seriously.

He was irrepressible, Catriona thought, listening to him comment on his brother's likely reaction to the loss of what had obviously been an expensive dinghy, but Tim seemed to look upon its loss as being of no more import than a broken toy.

His attitude hadn't changed later when he was relating the events of the afternoon to the others over dinner. He shrugged aside Brett's enquiries as to his knowledge of the local currents with a rueful grin, and flirted outrageously with both herself and Fiona; probably with a slight bias towards her, Catriona acknowledged, but that was possibly because in Brett he sensed a formidable opponent.

He had spoken to his brother in Lerwick, and from the cheerful expression on his face when the call was over the loss of the dinghy was of scant importance.

'Old Alan will tear a strip off me later,' he told them. 'He's sending the chopper over for me first thing tomorrow morning and then I'm to be banished back to London. He claims I'm not safe.' He assumed an air of injured innocence totally at variance with the wicked twinkle in his eyes. 'One of the penalties of working for the family firm. Big brother is quite definitely the boss.' He had already told them about the small air freight business his brother ran to the islands and the rigs, and Catriona could not help thinking that she would be reluctant to entrust her life to the hands of this attractive but quite feckless young man. Even the rather pointed rebuffs Fiona kept administering failed to dent his exuberance.

'What do you do for night life round here?' he asked when they were all sitting down.

'We don't,' Magnus told him shortly. Catriona could sense that her brother did not like Tim. She had made up a bed for him in Tex's room. Because of the bad weather Brett had sent telegrams to the others warning them not to try to return to Falla until conditions improved, and listening to Tim commenting on the oddity of Falla's climate Catriona could not help contrasting him with Brett.

'Where does a guy take a pretty girl when he wants to whisper sweet nothings in her ear?' he asked Magnus, watching Catriona appreciatively. Magnus made some noncommittal comment, but Catriona felt her cheeks burn as she looked up and found Brett watching her with barely concealed anger. Surely he could not think that she would actively encourage Tim? But then of course why shouldn't he? she thought bitterly. He probably thought now that she was the type of girl who jumped in and out of bed with any man. Her response to him had been quite unmistakable, and he was not to know that it had been born of her intense love for him. She shuddered deeply. Far better that he thought her the very worst sort of amoral bed-hopper than guess the truth.

She had been sleeping badly ever since their return from the rig, and tonight the keening wind was particularly bothersome. When it woke her up for the third time she glanced at her alarm and sighed. Two o'clock. Her throat felt dry, and she got up, pulling on her old flannel dressing gown. A cup of tea might help her sleep.

She moved about the kitchen quietly, not wanting to wake the others, cradling the steaming mug in her hands as she hurried back to her room.

She didn't see the pyjamaed figure standing at the top of the stairs until she was almost on a level with it, and scalding tea slopped down over her hands as she jumped nervously.

'It's only me,' Tim reassured her. 'I was on my way to the bathroom and got lost.'

'Down the other end of the landing,' Catriona told him.

'Mmm, you look very tempting like this,' he murmured, making no attempt to step aside. 'Is your hair natural?' One arm slid round her waist as he spoke, his free hand touching her hair.

'Stop it, Tim!' she warned him. 'I don't play games . . .'

'Who says I'm playing?' His breath was fanning her ear and she tried to move out of his arms without either making any noise or spilling her tea, but he refused to let her go, laughing down into her indignant face.

'One kiss and I'll let you go,' he promised. 'I've been wanting to taste that delectable mouth ever since I first saw you.'

Trying to decide the safest course between creating a scene and disturbing the rest of the household, and making it quite plain to Tim that she had no

wish to enter into any flirtation with him, Catriona
pleaded with him to let her go.

It was a mistake. He merely laughed, his eyes
glinting with devilment as he ran his hand lightly
along her arm.

'Poor Cat!' he teased. 'Yell at me and big brother
will be out here demanding to know my intentions.
Just one small kiss,' he coaxed. 'Can't you spare just
one?'

'If you don't let me go I shall pour this tea all
over you,' Catriona warned him evenly. 'I mean it,
Tim . . .'

'Do you now . . .' His mouth hovered purposefully
above hers, and she tensed automatically, determined to rebuff him. A sudden shaft of light illumi-
nated the landing as a bedroom door was thrust
open, and with a sinking heart Catriona realised that
it was Brett's. They must have disturbed him. His
expression when he saw Catriona in Tim's arms and
their mutual state of undress was like a knife right
through her heart.

'Unless you want to rouse the whole household I
suggest you find somewhere a little more private,' he
said bitingly, his glance sweeping Catriona's tumbled
curls and pale cheeks, as Tim, for once losing some
of his exuberance, quickly released her.

'Are you speaking from experience?' Catriona
whipped back, hoping the probing eyes wouldn't
guess the reason for her bitter defiance.

His eyes withered her.

'Not the sort you were just indulging in.'

'Phew!' Tim commented feelingly when Brett's
door-had closed behind him. 'And I thought big
brother was tough! Hey, come on, surely it can't be
as bad as that,' he protested when two large tears

rolled down Catriona's cheeks, breaking through her self-control. 'Oh, I get it,' he exclaimed softly when she didn't speak. 'Like that, is it? Well, I wish you luck, little mermaid. At a guess I'd say Brett Simons was a very hard man to cross.'

True to his word, Tim's brother arrived first thing in the morning, refusing Catriona's offer of a cup of coffee and looking none too pleased with his unrepentant relative.

'Sorry you've been put to so much trouble,' he apologised to Magnus. 'It was damned lucky for Tim that your fisherman was there to pull him to safety. I'd warned him not to take the dinghy out alone. Anyone with the slightest bit of sense knows these waters are lethal.'

Tim's brother was considerably older than Tim, and from what Tim had told them the previous evening Catriona guessed that Tim had been spoiled appallingly by his parents. His total lack of any sense of responsibility or remorse went a long way to detract from his sunny nature. He insisted on kissing Catriona before climbing into the helicopter, and she could feel Brett's eyes on them.

'Young idiot,' Magnus commented briefly when they had gone. 'He's lucky to be alive, but to talk to him you'd never think he'd been in any danger.'

'I've had a word with his brother about transporting us to and from Lerwick for the festival,' Brett commented. 'I hope that's okay?'

'Fine by me,' Magnus assured him.

Brett looked at Catriona. She took a deep breath.

'If you don't mind, I think I'll give it a miss this year.' She sedulously avoided meeting Brett's eyes. Let him think what he liked, she wasn't going to put herself through the agony of watching him with

Fiona. 'I'm thinking of returning to London,' she added wildly when Magnus raised an eyebrow, 'taking up my course again. I . . . I . . . want to have some time to think about it.'

CHAPTER NINE

THE westering sun slid behind the banked clouds, tinging them the iridescent, uncapturable shades of mother-of-pearl. It sank slowly to the sea, turning the waves blood red and then molten ochre, drawing Catriona's awed eyes, even though she had seen the phenomenon many, many times before.

'Quite something, these northern sunsets,' Brett commented from her elbow. She didn't speak to him. She was still licking her wounds from their confrontation this morning. By rights she should not be in this helicopter winging its way to Lerwick, but at home on Falla. Where she would have been if Brett hadn't cornered her in the kitchen, demanding that she accompany the others to the main island.

'Why?' she had demanded. 'So that you and Fiona needn't be burdened with Magnus? Three's a crowd and all that. Why don't you simply tell him, or are you frightened of him backing out of the terminal?'

His mouth had compressed then, harsh lines scored either side of his mouth as his self-control was stretched to its limits.

'You're coming,' he had told her forcefully, 'even if I have to drag you screaming all the way.'

Brett she could have defied, but when Magnus

came to her and asked to go with them, him she could not refuse.

'I know how you feel, Cat.' His assurance was accompanied by a brief grimace. 'And how! Come on, Cat, why spoil their happiness?'

'Well, if you can do it, so can I.' But her shaky claim belied her doubts that she could endure the particularly agonising type of torture Magnus was suggesting.

The sun finally slid beneath the waves and Catriona switched her thoughts to the present.

'The hotel first, and then dinner,' Brett suggested smoothly, opening the rear door of a hire car to allow Fiona and Catriona to slide inside.

'I expect you two girls will want to freshen up,' he added, glancing backwards as he unclipped his seat belt.

Catriona frowned. She hadn't brought anything particularly dressy. The Up-Helly-Aa was essentially an outdoors celebration with much roistering and merriment in the streets of Lerwick, and apart from the dark, well fitting cords she was wearing in place of her normal jeans, all she had in her overnight bag was a change of underclothes, a short sheepskin jacket, a lace blouse and the slim-fitting black velvet skirt experience had told her covered most occasions. With her cords she was wearing a soft angora jumper in her favourite shade of lilac to complement her subtle eye make-up. The pilot of the helicopter had done a double-take as he jumped down to help her in, but Brett had barely looked at her. She knew it wasn't merely vanity to think she was attractive. Her hair alone would have earned her more than one look from most men without the delicate purity of her bone structure, and her slim, softly curved body.

But of course looks weren't everything; merely the packaging.

'Here we are.'

She stared up at the hotel in horror, turning accusingly to Brett, who was calmly stepping out of the car.

'I can recommend this place personally,' he was drawling as he removed the luggage from the boot. 'Their service is quite unique.'

'Yes, it's a small family-run business,' Magnus interposed, unaware of the hidden meaning beneath the comment. 'They're very keen on personal service.'

'So I seem to recall,' Brett agreed, looking at Catriona in a way which brought the colour to her face. 'They were fairly fully booked, and all I could get was two doubles, I'm afraid,' he added.

There was an uncomfortable silence. Catriona looked at Magnus. He was white beneath his tan, and she guessed they shared the same thought. Who would be sharing with whom?

'Something wrong?' Brett asked Catriona suavely.

'Not really.' She gave him a saccharine smile. 'I was just remembering a particularly unpleasant experience. Something I'm trying hard to forget.'

'Or not remembering with honesty,' he mocked. 'Okay with you if we give the girls first choice of the rooms, Magnus?' he called over his shoulder.

There was nothing in Fiona's expression to show whether she was relieved or disappointed by this comment. In the other girl's shoes there would be no doubt about her feelings, Catriona thought enviously. She would have been downright disappointed. But perhaps when one knew that one's love was reciprocated it did not burn quite as fiercely. She looked a little more closely at Fiona. The other girl seemed to have lost weight, and her eyes did not have the unquenchable sparkle of a girl deep in love who knows that her love is returned.

The rooms were pretty much identical. Brett had booked them a table at a local restaurant. They were eating early so that they would not miss any of the festivities, and while she waited for Fiona to emerge from the bathroom Catriona studied her complexion in the mirror. The pure air of the Shetlands had given her skin a bloom it had lacked in London, but her eyes were shadowed. She was a far more mature twenty-two now than she had been before she returned to Falla; in more ways than one, she acknowledged wryly. Never again would she underestimate the power of physical desire.

'Bathroom's all yours,' Fiona announced, opening the bedroom door. There was a constraint between them which had never been there during their adolescence. Had Fiona guessed how she felt about Brett?

She showered quickly and hurried back to the bedroom. Fiona was wearing a soft tweed skirt that suited her colouring, toned with a Shetland wool sweater. She was applying lipstick when Catriona walked in and smiled at her in the mirror.

The velvet skirt was slacker on the waist than Catriona remembered, but she didn't think anyone would notice.

'Suits you,' Fiona approved when she had finished dressing. 'You and Magnus both have such distinctive colouring. Every time I see a blond head in Edinburgh I automatically think of him.' She flushed suddenly, biting her lip, as though regretting the admission. 'If you're ready, shall we go down?'

Without giving Catriona an opportunity to reply

she opened the door. Magnus and Brett were walking along the landing, Brett dressed in dark hip-hugging pants and a soft white skirt, carelessly buttoned to reveal his chest and throat, a leather jacket slung over one arm.

'Good timing!' His smile for Fiona was warm. Catriona glanced hesitantly at her brother. He was dressed similarly to Brett but to her eyes lacked the other man's powerful aura of male sensuality; invisible, but so potent that her senses reacted to it involuntarily.

The restaurant was within easy walking distance of the hotel—Catriona had been relieved to discover that the girl who had booked her in on her last visit was not on the desk. She had no wish to be reminded of that particular night.

The head waiter met them as they walked through the small bar. The restaurant was full; oilmen greatly in evidence and obviously very much prepared to enjoy the evening's entertainment. As they had walked past the cloakroom Catriona had been amused by the number of soft felt Stetsons perched on pegs above leather jackets. Oilmen might be casual in their attire, but it was an expensive casualness.

Without hesitation they all opted for lobster for their first course. Catriona shook her head to the wine waiter, but Brett overruled her.

'Half a glass won't do you any harm. Quite the contrary.'

Catriona chose chicken Kiev for her main course. It was delicious, but she barely touched a mouthful. Outside the streets were filling up with locals and visitors alike determined to take part in the festivities.

'Exactly what happens?' Brett queried when they had reached the coffee stage.

'In essence the festival is Viking in origin,' Magnus explained, 'and had existed in Lerwick for many centuries, but in the 1880s a local man—Haldane Burgess—developed the present-day celebrations out of the traditional life-renewing fire festivals. Then they used to roll barrels of burning tar through the streets, but nowadays they re-construct a Viking longboat which is ceremoniously burned.'

'Like a funeral boat?' Brett interrupted knowledgeably.

Magnus nodded. 'To the ancient Vikings fire signified the renewal of life, and Up-Helly-Aa reinforces the belief in "new life". The men dress up in costumes—guisers, we call them—and the Bill is stuck up in the market square—that would have been done first thing this morning. Basically it's a written recap of all the previous year's gossip, but in reality the longer and funnier the story the better. Then the guisers spend the day visiting the local communities, schools etc. It's considered quite a feat to exchange badinage with a guiser and come off best. In the evening there's a procession through the streets. It's quite breathtaking, awesome in some respects, as they drag the longboat to its final resting place and burning.

After that all hell breaks loose,' Magnus warned with a grin. 'You've heard all about Scotsmen with a few drinks inside them—well, wait until you see the Shetlanders! They work hard and they play hard. In theory each group of guisers visits every one of the half dozen or so halls in Lerwick entertaining the crowds, and only when each troupe has entertained every hall can they go home.'

'Sounds as though we're going to need some stamina to see it through,' Brett commented.

Magnus laughed.

'Do you remember the first year we were allowed to see one through, Cat?'

How could she forget it? It had been the year before their parents' accident.

'I insisted on having two lots of candy-floss and was quite dreadfully sick,' she agreed reminiscently.

'So you did. I'd forgotten about that.'

'I'm surprised you can remember anything about it,' Catriona told him scathingly. 'All you had eyes for was that girl you brought home with you. What was her name? Miranda . . .'

'Oh God, yes, Miranda. I'd forgotten all about her. Nice girl,' he added with a grin.

If Magnus was going down he certainly intended to go down with all his flags flying, she thought. And she would do well to follow his example.

The evening was cool rather than cold. The wind had dropped, and snuggled inside her sheepskin Catriona felt deliciously warm. Revellers already thronged the streets, a holiday air very much in evidence. The smell of hot dogs—so much more enticing in the open air—wafted across the packed square.

'This way,' Magnus urged, taking the lead. 'I know a spot where we can get a first-hand view of everything.'

The streets were so crowded that it was impossible to walk four abreast. Catriona hurried forward to catch up with Magnus, but Brett grasped her arm, jerking her backwards.

'Magnus, in view of the crowds I think it might be better if we split into two pairs.'

Magnus paused, and Catriona tried to pull away from Brett to go to him.

'Stay right where you are.' The gritted command startled her, but even more startled was the look Fiona gave Brett as she moved hesitantly towards Magnus.

'What did you do that for?' Catriona demanded angrily as her brother and Fiona were swallowed up by the vast crowd.

'Perhaps I just wanted to give them a chance to recapture whatever it was they had and lost.'

For a moment sheer incredulity held her rigid, and then, her eyes bitter, she said in a voice that shook with rage:

'I get it!' Her lip curled faintly with contempt. 'But you needn't have been so self-sacrificing, Magnus is already quite prepared to let you go ahead with the terminal. Have you asked Fiona how she feels about this turn and turn about, though? She might not see it in quite the same light as you. After all, she has nothing to gain, has she?'

'Why, you . . . you despicable little bitch!' His savagery stunned her.

'Me despicable?' she said ungrammatically. 'What about you? First you steal Magnus's girl-friend, and then when it suits your book you hand her right back to him . . .'

'Fiona . . .'

'Fiona must be besotted with you to let you get away with it,' Catriona interrupted heatedly. 'I don't know what she possibly sees in you. You're arrogant . . . unscrupulous . . . unfeeling . . . u. . . .'

'Have you quite finished?'

She was lifted off her feet, her eyes suddenly and alarming on a level with Brett's.

'Put me down!' she raged impotently.

'And miss an opportunity to prove just how despicable I can be? Fiona and Magnus are watching us.' His lips twisted in a mocking smile. 'Unless you want Fiona to take your place, you'd better just go along with me, Catriona Peterson.'

He was despicable, she fulminated ten seconds later, and not only that, but knowledgeable and experienced as well, because instead of resisting the harsh pressure of his punishing lips as she knew they ought, her own were parting mindlessly for them, her soft moan of pleasure at the feel of his body against her, imprisoning her between his flesh and the solid wall behind them, bringing triumph to the eyes that searched her unguarded face.

'Despicable or not, you want me!' he cried harshly. 'And God knows if we weren't standing here in this crowd I'd be tempted to show you here and now just how much!' His hand slid mockingly along her body, inviting her to deny its instinctive response. Unable to bear the mockery in his eyes, she turned away.

'I'm tired of listening to your insults, Catriona,' he said softly. 'It's high time you learned that you can't just behave as you like and not face the consequences.'

Her legs had turned to jelly. No, not jelly, she thought wildly, that had some substance. To cotton-wool; and only Brett's arms prevented her from falling at his feet.

'The consequences?' Her voice trembled huskily, her tongue touching her dry lips defensively.

'Not feeling quite so brave now, are we?' Brett mocked. The crowd had started to move away, following the procession. 'Come with me . . .'

'Where are you taking me?'

'Where do you think?' came the silky response. 'I've been deprived of my woman—albeit in a good cause, and despicable creature that I am, I want a substitute . . .'

'Then find another one!' Catriona protested wildly. 'You can't force me to go with you . . .'

'You're forgetting this is Up-Helly-Aa night,' Brett insisted softly. 'We'll just be mistaken for another couple of revellers. I could walk through the streets with you in my arms and no one would stop me. No, this is the ideal solution—an eye for an eye, a tooth for a tooth, a woman for a woman . . . Unless of course you want me to take Fiona from Magnus again? Think of it as a penance,' he mocked, 'a way of repaying your brother for all his past generosity. After all, it won't be as though you're giving me anything you haven't already given someone else, will it?' His glance flicked her contemptuously. 'I shouldn't have thought Tim much of a lover . . .'

'You'd be surprised.' Somehow she had to escape from him. Even now she couldn't believe that he meant to put his threats into practice, but the look in his eyes warned her that he did.

Trembling with mingled fear and outrage, she hung back as he started to lead her back to the hotel. At one point his grasp of her wrist slackened enough for her to pull free, which she did, bolting round a corner, only to run head on into two burly revellers, obviously the worse for drink. They probably meant no harm, but on top of what she had just endured their alcohol-laden breath and determined grasp of her arm petrified her, and she was almost glad to be relinquished to Brett's guardianship.

'Very wise,' was his only comment.

Her last hope that someone would stop them in the hotel reception was banished when she discovered that it was completely empty. Everyone with the slightest excuse for being there was out on the streets.

The room Brett took her to contained two single beds, and bore no resemblance to the one they had shared that first night, but nevertheless the memories came flooding back.

'Brett . . . please don't do this,' she pleaded as he locked the door and withdrew the key. 'I'm sorry if I made you angry . . .'

'You will be,' he assured her grimly removing his jacket. His shirt followed it on to the bed, revealing the taut smoothness of his torso to her terrified gaze. Beautiful, she had called him. Lethal, would have been a better description. Tonight he was all animal grace and ferocity, and she knew that whatever she found in his arms would leave her scarred and bleeding for the rest of her life.

'Don't just stand there,' he ordered coolly. 'Or are you waiting for me to undress you? Is that what you like, Catriona?' He had come to stand over her, his breath wafting the tendrils of hair curling round her face. 'Well, it's what I like that matters tonight. And what I should like is to hear you begging me to make love to you.'

'Never!'

'You don't learn, do you?'

He reached for her with the soft words, and her unyielding, tense body was drawn within the circle of his arms, his hand reaching for the zipper on her skirt. It slithered to the floor and she was lifted clear of it and carried to the narrow single bed.

'Small, but it will serve our purpose. After all, we

won't be sleeping together, will we? Merely exchanging a mutual payment of debts. What's wrong?' he added in that same soft tone. 'I seem to remember the last time I held you in my arms like this you told me I was "beautiful".'

'No!' She tried to shut the words out, but he removed her hands from her ears, no compassion in the eyes that stripped away her pitiful defences.

'Oh, come on,' he chided. 'A girl of your experience and ... appetites ... isn't embarrassed by a little thing like that. Did you find Tim "beautiful" too?' he demanded with a sudden savagery.

'Yes!'

Catriona flung the words at him in angry self-defence, her eyes blurring with tears, which did nothing to shield her from the fury leaping into his face.

'And you have the gall to criticise me!'

His mouth covered hers before she could protest, its cold pressure a ravishment of the tender, vulnerable flesh. She was crying when he lifted his head, but he took no notice of the soundless tears sliding on to the pillow, his hands busy with her blouse and brief underthings.

'So perfect ... and so flawed ...'

He bent his head and she saw the desire leaping to life in his eyes. That terrified her more than anything else that had happened, because while she had not been able to believe that he would take her simply in cold anger, his desire could fuel her own and once that deep aching chord of need coiled inside her came to life she would not be able to prevent herself from doing exactly what he wanted and begging him for fulfilment.

That knowledge splintered the last of her brittle

self-control. As his hands explored her body she trembled like an aspen newly exposed to a raw east wind.

'It's no use, Catriona,' Brett warned her, lifting his mouth from its downward exploration of her body. 'I won't be swayed. I mean to have you whether you enjoy it or not . . .'

'Five minutes ago you were saying that I would be begging you to make love to me,' she reminded him. Words were her only defence now; somehow she must kill his desire with the sharpness of her tongue. 'Why the sudden change? Or are you ready to admit that you can't arouse me?'

'Oh, I can arouse you all right,' he said lazily. 'But right now I've got more important things on my mind.' He glanced significantly at his own un-ashamedly aroused body. 'Why should I bother about satisfying a selfish bitch like you? Although I might do . . . later,' he added in a husky voice, 'just to prove to you that I can.'

His mouth was against her breast and to her ever-lasting shame she felt it flower into pulsating life, delight mingling with the fear coiled deep inside her. This was not how she wanted it to be, she thought miserably. She wanted tenderness . . . concern . . . and most of all love!

Brett moved, thrusting one leg between hers, forc-ing them apart, and her body tensed in rejection. Terrified panic had taken the place of desire.

'Brett, please don't do this,' she pleaded again. 'I'm not . . . I . . .'

'You're not what?' he mocked, taking her face between his hands. 'Ready to join me on the most exciting journey any two human beings can take together? Why should I care? I'm going to be

damned in eternal hell fire from now on anyway.'
The last few words were muttered under his breath,
and she only just caught them.

'Because you've given Fiona up to Magnus . . .
You don't have to, you know. Magnus will still back
the scheme.'

'But will you? One agreement's no use without the
other. No, I've made my decision, and there's no
going back. Not for either of us.'

His mouth touched hers, a curious expression in
his eyes as he looked into her frozen face.

'Don't look at me like that, damn you!' he swore.
'You came to life in my arms before, and you will do
again. You will do, Catriona,' he threatened softly.
'Don't ever doubt it.'

The pressure of his mouth had changed and with
the change came the alarm bells ringing in her brain,
for now it was subtly caressing, stroking and coaxing,
making her ache to return the caress, to press herself
against his hard masculinity and feel her flesh dis-
solving. She moaned a protest, but he ignored her
his lips on the exposed column of her throat, making
her feel almost faint with the pleasure he was evok-
ing. Her own lips, burning and dry, ignored the
signals from her brain; all lucid thought was suspen-
ded as they pressed hot kisses against his flesh,
savouring the tangy male taste of him and feeling his
muscles clench beneath her assault. When she
touched his body, he muttered something under his
breath, guiding her hands to the buckle of his belt,
urging her inexperienced fingers to remove the final
barrier so that her flesh could touch his and feel his
demanding masculinity with mingled fear and excitement.

Some deep primeval need inside her urged consummation, demanded her total sacrifice of heart, body and soul. Her body felt languorously boneless, the harsh rasping of his body hair against the softness of her skin heightening her sensual awareness. Brett claimed her lips in fierce possession, his body moving against her. Another moment and . . .

A cold sweat filmed her body. What was she *doing*? With eyes that widened in panic she searched his face for some sign of caring. There was none. She pushed him away and heard his hoarsely muttered, 'God, no . . . not . . .' before he rolled away from her, his body convulsing.

'God, you really know how to emasculate a man, don't you? There's a name for women like you!' He said it crudely, watching her whiten with shock. 'And don't give me any of that mock innocent stuff. I saw you with Tim, remember? Now get out of here,' he said tiredly, 'before I forget that I'm a man and not an animal.'

It was late when Fiona came back. She was humming under her breath, and Catriona feigned sleep. How could Fiona sound so happy when she loved Brett? A sudden thought struck her. Could Brett have left the hotel and found the other two? Perhaps taken Fiona away from Magnus a second time? Had Fiona too known the savage mastery of his touch?

CHAPTER TEN

'AND you'll definitely come back and be Fiona's bridesmaid?' Magnus demanded.

They were in the library. They had just returned from seeing Fiona off. Catriona had pretended an absorbing interest in the skyline to give the two lovers an opportunity to say their goodbyes. Ever since their return from Lerwick Magnus and Fiona had been inseparable.

Catriona still wasn't sure exactly what had happened between them. Perhaps Fiona, more sensible than she was, had realised what poor husband material Brett was. No, that wasn't being entirely fair to Fiona, she acknowledged. The other girl was obviously deeply in love with Magnus.

'You're still determined to leave at the end of the week, then?' Magnus pressed.

She had to. Brett was still on Falla and there was a limit to how long she could endure to remain in such close contact with him, his presence constantly eroding her fragile self-control.

'Still feel the same?' Magnus sympathised. 'I won't trot out any platitudes about time being the great healer. But I am sorry.'

Magnus was going down to the voe where Brett was busy working, and driven by a need to be alone, she packed a small haversack and set off up the hill, as they called the steeply rising mountain behind the house.

At the top it levelled out into the grassy plateau

where the first lairds of Falla had built their castle from stone quarried on the island.

She had packed a flask of soup, sandwiches, and a large bar of chocolate, but her appetite had deserted her. All she could think of, over and over again, was her last confrontation with Brett. She was lying on the peat, looking out over the sea, and she rolled over on to her back, studying the fast moving formation of the clouds. It was sheltered here behind the crumbling stone walls of the old castle, and the sleep which had eluded her for so many nights lately slipped over her so gently that she wasn't even aware of her eyes closing.

The mist rolling in from the sea woke her. She sat up shivering with cold and damp, furious with herself for being so careless. The mist was so thick she could barely see her hand in front of her face, never mind the sandstone castle walls. She took a pace forward, alarmed when the turf broke away beneath her. She knew this island like the back of her hand, but she had still unthinkingly stepped towards the sharp cliff edge and could quite easily have fallen over it into the turbulent seas below.

Mist blanketed the island like thick grey wool. Trying to get her bearings, Catriona forced herself to concentrate on projecting a mental picture of her surroundings. No one knew she was up here. The mist had rolled in while she slept, and already the light was fading. Magnus and Brett must surely have returned to the house, but even if they were already aware that she was missing, they would not have the slightest idea where to find her. She had ignored all the most basic laws of survival, she fretted, furious with her own stupidity. Falla was perhaps not very large, but it still might be several hours before she could return home; several hours when Magnus would be worrying unnecessarily about her.

After half an hour when the mist showed no signs of lifting and her jeans and jacket were soaked through with its clammy touch, she made up her mind. If she was very careful she might be able to find the path and follow it downwards. The only trouble was that it was rarely used, and while her feet had found it easily enough in the daylight, with night coming on and the mist pressing down she would literally have to find her way blind. It was an unnerving prospect, especially when she ~ remembered how steeply the ground sloped in places and the marshy ground she would have to cover where the track levelled out next to the loch.

She didn't have much choice, she reminded herself. A night spent out here, exposed to the elements, could well result in severe exposure, if nothing else, and again she cursed her own stupidity in not letting Magnus know where she was going.

Carefully feeling her way, she slipped and slithered down the winding path, guided more by instinct than anything else. The sound of running water warned her of danger once, as she came perilously close to plunging into the burn which fed the inland loch.

The first time she heard the faint echo of her name, she thought she was imagining things, and froze, vainly trying to pierce the stifling grey blanket.

Her ears, more finely attuned this time, caught the sound again, closer now, and with her heart thudding with relief she cupped her hands together and called back.

Within moments the faint scrabbling of paws heralded the arrival of Russet, tongue lolling, tail feathering the air, as he barked his discovery.

A little later Magnus and Findlay emerged through the gloom, flashing a powerfully-beamed torch carefully around them. As Magnus hugged her shivering body to him, Catriona leant her forehead against his chest in a gesture of total gratitude.

'Don't say anything! I already know what an utter fool I am. My only excuse is that I fell asleep.'

Far from being angry, Magnus was oddly tender.

'Don't worry about it,' he comforted her. 'I guessed when you didn't turn up at teatime that you'd have headed for the castle.'

Another figure was emerging from the gloom, and Catriona's heart did a double somersault as she saw Brett. The damp had plastered his dark hair to his skull, and for a moment her legs turned to water as she contemplated how wonderful it would have been to be able to go into his arms as freely as she did her brother's.

'You are clever!' She wasn't really paying much attention to Magnus. All the yearning love buried inside her strained towards Brett.

'Not really.'

Brett had drawn level with them now, and she searched his face hungrily for some sign of softening of his hard contempt.

'You're forgetting,' Magnus chided her gently, 'I found you there after . . . after Mum and Dad, and in the circumstances I guessed you'd headed straight here.'

Brett wasn't looking at her. Misery enveloped her. She ought to be feeling relieved that soon she would be leaving Falla, but all she could feel was pain.

'Let's get you home.' Magnus stripped off his thick

jacket and wrapped it round her. 'You're soaked through!'

Memories of another occasion when Brett had said something similar tore at her with red-hot claws. The thought of his hands on her body as he slowly rubbed her dry would not be denied, and desire swept weakening over her, making her falter hesitantly, turning to Magnus with anguished eyes as he turned to steady her.

The rest of the journey was only a blur—Russet's excited barking, Findlay's gruff voice, Magnus's gentle and compassionate as he hurried her into the warm kitchen and into the chair before the fire.

'I wish Fiona was here,' he commented at one point, eyeing her tragic face.

'Oh, I'll be fine.' She had caused him enough worry. 'A hot bath and a good night's sleep and I'll be like new.'

Brett hadn't said a word. He was leaning on the kitchen door, drinking tea, his hair starting to curl slightly as it dried. It made him look less austere, more approachable, and for a moment she was tormented by a wild longing to go to him and rest her aching head on his shoulder. So overwhelming was the impulse that she had to fight to remind herself of what he really was, of how ruthlessly he actually used people and situations to meet his own ends.

'Come on, time you were in bed,' Magnus announced, removing the mug from her chilled fingers. 'And don't bother getting up in the morning. Brett and I are flying to Aberdeen for talks about the terminal.'

'When will you be back?'

'I don't know.' He looked at Brett, who prised himself away from the door and shrugged carelessly.

'I've got some business to attend to and I may stay over until next week.' His eyes avoided hers.

'So this is goodbye?' She was quite proud of how carefully she managed to control her voice. She knew that she would have been leaving at the end of the week anyway, but somehow, coming like this, on top of her ordeal, the news that this was the last time she would see him caught her unprepared. Her lips trembled and she looked away from him, conscious of the comforting pressure of Magnus's hand on her shoulder.

'Looks like it.' The casual tone suggested that it didn't matter to him particularly either way.

'You'll be coming back for the wedding, though, and of course, once the terminal gets the go-ahead,' Magnus said easily.

But by then she would be in London, Catriona thought feverishly. Her whole body seemed to be in the grip of a paralysing fear. Every instinct urged her to beg him to stay, to forcibly prevent him from leaving if need be, but pride restrained her—a fierce, foolish pride which blurred her eyes with the tears she would not shed, and forced her to smile vaguely and wish him well for the future.

Her wish was reciprocated, equally formally; there was not even to be the last bitter-sweet pain of a goodbye kiss, which would have been treasured, no matter how casual.

She was awake before the men, and lay listening to their preparations, hoping against hope that Brett would come in to say goodbye. When the bedroom door was eventually pushed open, only Magnus came in.

'I'm fine,' she assured him in response to his anxious query. 'Quite well enough to be out of bed. I ought really to be doing my own packing.'

'Leave it until I get back. I'll phone you to let you know when I'm leaving. Just try and rest today. Read some of those paperbacks you bought for me, and stay in bed. Understood?'

She nodded slowly, too drained and lethargic to argue. She had had no idea that love could make you feel so ill, she reflected wryly.

The men had gone, and she was completely alone. She read for a while and then discarded the book, her own train of thought too disruptive to permit her to concentrate.

Images of Brett filled her mind to the exclusion of all else. It no longer seemed to matter that he had made use of them, that he had put expediency above all else, that he had quite unequivocally rejected him; she loved him.

She surfaced from a light doze to find that evening was closing in. There had been no call from Magnus, and she was beginning to feel hungry. She was just about to get dressed when the unmistakable sound of a helicopter broke the early evening silence.

Magnus! Obviously he had been able to get away earlier than he thought and had come straight home. She sat up eagerly in her bed, waiting for the familiar sound of the kitchen door opening, her hair cascading over her shoulders as she drew her knees up under her chin.

She heard footsteps on the stairs which suddenly seemed to hesitate and she called out, thinking that perhaps her brother thought she might be sleeping and not want to disturb her.

'It's okay, Magnus, I'm awake,' she called impatiently. 'Come and tell me all about it.'

The door opened and the expectancy died out of her face.

'Brett!' His name was a shocked whisper, for a moment the creamy flesh revealed by her thin silk nightgown forgotten as she stared disbelievingly up at the man standing by the door. In a dark business suit he seemed taller and broader, and far less approachable than at any time before. Half an inch of crisp white shirt cuff protruded beneath the immaculately tailored cloth, emphasising the tanned masculine hands.

'What . . . what . . . what are you doing here?' she managed at last, suddenly conscious of her shiny unmade-up face and tangled hair. 'I thought you weren't coming back.'

'I changed my mind,' he said smoothly. He was watching her with an expression she could not define. 'I had some unfinished business.'

She didn't enquire what it was. The full realisation that he had returned was just beginning to have its effect upon her.

'You look pale,' he said abruptly. 'Have you had any food today?' She shook her head, too dazed to speak.

'Stay there. I'll bring you something.'

'I can get up,' she started to protest, but he frowned, making her unwary pulses race in dismay. Perhaps he didn't want to eat with her? Yes, that must be it.

'What would you like?'

'Whatever you're having,' she said indifferently. She wasn't interested in food, only in his company.

'I've already eaten.' The brusque response hurt. She was a tiresome chore he had taken over from Magnus. Where was her brother? she wondered suddenly. As though he had read her thoughts Brett supplied the answer. 'After the meeting was over

Magnus decided to go down to Edinburgh and see Fiona.'

'Was the meeting successful?' She didn't really care one way or the other, all she was doing was prolonging the inevitable moment when he would leave her.

'From your point of view or mine?' he asked dryly, wandering over to her bedside and picking up the book she was reading. It was one of the latest best-sellers and she had bought it primarily for Magnus. She had read half a dozen chapters without taking in anything and was disconcerted when Brett made some comment on the plot.

'Er—yes, I suppose so,' she agreed. 'To tell the truth, my mind wasn't on it properly.'

'No.' He placed the book down again, carefully straightening the spine. 'What was it on, then?'

'You still haven't told me about the meeting.' Avoidance seemed to be her best method of defence. There was no way she could admit that he had occupied her thoughts to the exclusion of all else.

'Oh yes, the meeting. We've got tentative approval for the terminal, provided you and Magnus agree, of course. There are still one or two ends to be tied up, but I think I managed to satisfy them that the voe was admirably suited for our purpose. It was a lucky day for me when I came to Falla.'

'But not for me!'

His eyebrows rose, but there was none of the anger she had come to expect in response to such challenging remarks.

'I had noticed,' he agreed dryly, glancing at his watch. 'How does scrambled eggs and toast sound?'

'There's really no need to bother.' She hunted round for her robe which had been on the end of the bed. 'I'm sure you must have an awful lot to do, packing and so forth, I'll go downstairs later and make myself something.'

'It's no bother,' he contradicted. 'Now stay there like a good girl while I go and make it.'

He was gone before she could object, and she heard him whistling as he ran downstairs. She had seen him in varying moods during their acquaintanceship, but never one like this. He seemed almost lighthearted—relief perhaps that matters were progressing with the terminal. Yes, that must be it, she acknowledged. No doubt he was feeling far too pleased with life to pursue his dislike of her.

When he returned with the tray she was sitting by her fire in her robe, her hair brushed and a faint slick of lip gloss colouring her mouth. There was something about being in bed while he stood there fully dressed in his executive suit that made her feel very much at a disadvantage.

The toast and eggs looked delicious and her mouth watered. There was also a pot of tea—and two cups. She glanced at him uncertainly.

'I'm not hungry, but I am thirsty,' he said smoothly. 'So it's a June wedding for Magnus and Fiona.'

Magnus had not commented to her about Brett's relationship with Fione and she had not wanted to pry. Now she allowed a little of her jealousy to surface and asked casually, 'Do you want to change places with him?'

'I wouldn't mind a June wedding,' he replied urbanely, purposely misunderstanding her question. There was no way she could pry any further, but the thought of him with Fiona caused her such pain that her appetite vanished completely. She pushed her plate away, not caring what interpretation he might place on the betraying gesture.

'Tea?'

She nodded her head tiredly. Suddenly all she wanted was for him to go, and leave her completely in peace.

He poured it, handing her the cup, their fingers touched, and an electric charge shot through her.

'By the way,' he said casually, 'Magnus tells me you're in love with me. Are you?'

If he hadn't been holding the cup she would have dropped it. A thousand emotions jostled for supremacy, uppermost astonishment that Magnus could have betrayed her so completely.

'Good heavens, no!' How light and careless her voice sounded. She must possess hidden dramatic talents she knew nothing about! 'He must have been teasing you.' Really, she marvelled at her own self-control.

'Must he?' There was a new, deep timbre to his voice. The tea-cup had been replaced on the tray, which was firmly moved aside as Brett bent over her, his hands either side of her body, imprisoning her within the chair. 'Well, there's only one way to find out.'

Passion she could have withstood, but not his gentle, almost teasing arousal of her body; these butterfly-light kisses being pressed upon her face and throat, leaving her aching for more; the strong male hands that without even touching her made her pulses throb with unappeased longing.

'Stop it, Brett!' she begged at one point, when his lips had touched hers in a caress too fleeting to quench her burning desire, but the light note she had managed so successfully before deserted her, and her voice cracked halfway through the command, the words emerging more as a pleading groan than a level-headed instruction.

'Stop what?' His tongue stroked over her lips, his hands grasping her firmly under the armpits so that every betraying tremor she made was instantly relayed to him.

Stop tormenting me like this, she wanted to say, but such an admission could never be made, not now. Too late, she admitted that it might have been wiser not to deny that she loved him. Better the clean, sharp humiliation she would have experienced then, that this slow, deliberate arousal of her senses, which threatened to tell him more plainly than any words exactly how she felt.

His thumbs stroked the soft flesh of her throat in a sensual circular movement and her lips parted on an audible sigh. His mouth brushed her face fleetingly—too fleetingly—his tongue probing the acutely sensitive area behind her ear. Her lips were clamped together to prevent the urgings of her body from becoming vocal. Another moment and she would be pleading incoherently for the satisfaction that only he could bring to her pulsating flesh. And then she knew on a sudden flash of intuition that that was exactly what he intended to do. And yet his touch was not angrily demanding as it had been on that other occasion; this time it was as though he was subtly telling her that he had all the time in the world—to take and give pleasure—and that he would not stop until he had reached the truth she was trying to conceal from him.

Another light kiss tortured her dry lips, and suddenly she could not fight him any longer. Her hands went up behind his neck, holding his mouth against her own, her lips trembling as her need rose up inside her like a tidal wave, refusing to be dammed by pride and convention any longer.

At first his lips remained cool, but he didn't move away, and then they began to move against hers; gently at first, as light as a puff of wind, the pressure gradually deepening, exploring the secret sweetness of her mouth until she was mindless with the sensations he was arousing, her fingers trembling against the buttons of his pristine white shirt, trying to seek the moist warmth of the flesh beneath.

He lifted her up and carried her to the bed, shedding his jacket with one lithe impatient movement, her robe parted by strong brown fingers to reveal the thrusting peaks of her breasts beneath their thin covering of silk.

She lay and watched him with eyes smoky with passion as his tie followed the jacket, her arms reaching upwards yearningly as he unfastened the top buttons of his shirt with sudden impatience.

His husky moan of arousal as her fingers touched his skin destroyed the last of her barriers. Her arms went round him, urging him against her, revelling in the hard pressure of his body, the abrasive sting of shadowed jaw as the silk nightdress was wrenched away jerkily and his dark head rested in the soft valley between her breasts. Pleasure flooded through her, peaking to unbearable excitement as his tongue caressed her skin, gently and then not so gently as his mouth closed hungrily over her nipple and her body burst into sudden urgent life, arching pleadingly beneath his, her finger nails raking the smooth skin of his back as she tried to communicate her need.

Suddenly denying that she loved him no longer

seemed to have much point. If they were going to make love, then let the word at least have some meaning. Let him remember her as foolish rather than free with her favours!

His arms curved her possessively against him, his expression hidden by the shadows, and for a moment she deluded herself that it held tenderness as well as the passion she had always hoped to find with her first lover. Brett her lover. Her whole body quivered. His flesh felt moist against hers; she reached up, letting her lips drift lingering over his skin, his shoulders, broad and hard, the powerful chest with its light covering of dark hair, tapering to a vee narrowing on to his flat stomach . . . Her lips followed the path of her errant fingers, until Brett jerked suddenly, hauling her against him and covering her mouth in fierce domination. There was no room for fear or regret; this was the moment she had been born for.

'Brett?'

He raised his head, searching her face in the darkness.

'Don't tell me you want me to stop, because I won't believe you.' He was breathing heavily, his muscles contracting in hurried urgency. 'And even if I did it's too damned late to do anything about it,' he muttered hoarsely. 'Oh, God . . . Cat . . .'

'I love you,' she said simply, close to tears. 'I didn't want you to know. I didn't want you to feel sorry for me. I . . .'

Tears blinded her as she was suddenly jerked upright and held away from him.

'I don't,' she was told uncompromisingly. 'I'm too busy feeling sorry for myself. Have you any idea what you've put me through? You with those huge violet eyes that always looked so disdainfully at me, and your silver-gilt hair, your body that nearly drives me mad with wanting you—mad enough to use force, something I've always despised in any human being towards the weak.'

She searched his face, hardly able to believe it wasn't all just a trick.

'No more arguments, no more misunderstanding, Cat,' he said unsteadily. 'I knew the first night we met that I'd fallen in love with you. Your looks knocked me for six—so small and fragile, and yet so sexy, but it wasn't just that. It was everything about you. Your pride, the way you stuck to your guns, not caring what I thought about you . . . or your outdated moral code . . .'

'But you said nothing . . . You let me go without . . .'

'Only because I knew you weren't going far,' Brett admitted wryly. 'I'd got it all worked out. So you didn't think much of me on first sight, but once I got to Falla I was pretty sure that I'd soon be able to wear down your resistance—to convince you just how right we were for one another, but it just didn't work out that way.' He grimaced slightly. 'In my arrogance I thought it would all be plain sailing, but in waters like these I ought to have known better.'

'I thought you were just trying to get round us, to make sure that the terminal went ahead,' Catriona admitted huskily. 'Every time you tried to help me or Magnus, I suspected you had some ulterior motive. I thought you were just being understanding about Magnus because you wanted to . . .'

'You shouldn't have thought any further than that,' he said softly. 'It was simply because I wanted you, full stop.'

'But you never said anything . . .'

'Not in words, perhaps.' His expression was wry. 'But surely the way I reacted to you physically must have told you something?'

'Only that you were aroused and angry.' She blushed a little under his teasing amusement.

'So innocent . . . and so infuriating! When I found you with Tim I didn't know whether to wring your neck there and then or carry you off to my bed and wring it when I made love to you until you were pleading with me for fulfilment—a fulfilment I was more than willing to give you,' he told her huskily. 'I never despised Magnus as you thought,' he added, suddenly serious. 'What happened to him is the kind of nightmare that haunts every man in our line of business. I did genuinely want to help him . . .'

'By stealing his girl-friend?'

'Fiona's idea. She was sure he was in love with her, but she knew his pride, knew that he would never make any approach to her while he continued to think himself worthless. All she wanted to do was to stir up a little natural jealousy. My fall from the rig did the rest. Am I right in thinking on that particular occasion you would have quite happily consigned me to the depths of the ocean?'

'Don't!' She shuddered deeply, laying her head against his shoulder. 'Don't talk about it,' she begged. 'Oh, Brett, I misjudged you so badly. When you criticised the food . . .'

'I thought you were deliberately trying to force us to leave. I have my pride too, my darling. Trying to get you to take notice of me was like battering my head against a brick wall. Although it might sound unbearably vain, until you happened along I hadn't had much trouble in the female companionship department.'

'Bighead!' Catriona teased, eyeing him possessively. There couldn't be many women who would not react to Brett's potent brand of male sensuality.

'When I discovered the truth from Mac, I felt about two inches tall. I couldn't wait to make amends, hence the freezer, but even that was thrown back in my face. I couldn't believe you would actually be fool enough to go out in that storm just to get meat. I knew you were physically attracted to me, but I was greedy, I wanted all of you, and yet knowing how unawakened you were I didn't want to force you . . . I told myself I would have to be patient, but you were so elusive. You're mine now, though,' he told her, looking along the length of her body with fierce possession. 'All of you.'

'Nearly all yours. But not quite,' she reminded him provocatively, breaking into a soft gurgle of laughter when he looked puzzled. Knowing that he loved her had given her new self-confidence, and she luxuriated in the way in which his eyes lingered on her skin and her body's immediate reaction.

'Surely you haven't forgotten already?' she teased. 'And you claiming to be so deeply in love with me!' She arched and stretched beneath his probing gaze, laughter in her eyes as Brett suddenly reached for her in comprehension.

'We'll see about that,' he announced determinedly, 'but first you have to pay for your other sins. I feel I deserve some form of recompense—like a hundred thousand kisses for every night I've spent lying alone in my bed dreaming of what it would be like to have you with me, to teach you to respond to me . . .' His eyes darkened as he looked at her slowly, faint colour high on his cheekbones, his pulse racing beneath her fingers.

'I thought I'd lost you,' he said thickly, no longer making any secret of his feelings. 'I think Magnus guessed how I felt. He kept on and on about you leaving and how unhappy you were. In the end I couldn't stop myself from asking why. I thought it might be the terminal—or Tim. When he told me you were in love with me, I just couldn't take it in.'

'You seemed pretty sure about it when you asked me. I nearly died of heart failure!'

'Mmm, if you had I'd have had to resuscitate you—like this,' he murmured, covering her mouth in a long drugging kiss. When he released her they were both breathing heavily.

'When you got lost in that mist, I knew I couldn't take any more. My control was dangerously near to breaking point last night. You'll never know how close I was to coming to your room and forcing you to respond to me.'

'Like you intended to do tonight,' Catriona teased gently.

'You can't know what it meant to me when Magnus told me that you loved me.'

'Show me,' she whispered against his mouth, the fierce desire rising up inside her to match his.

Several bliss-filled minutes later Brett released her to study her flushed, starry face.

'I'm not waiting until June for you, Cat,' he warned her huskily. 'I don't trust my self-control that far. Marry me soon.'

'Just as soon as you like.'

'We're not anticipating our marriage vows,' he told her gently. 'I want you—make no mistake about that, but I can wait. As long as you don't make me wait too long.'

She traced his crooked smile with one lazy fingertip. 'I don't want to wait at all,' she said softly, smiling as his arms closed round her. Somehow she thought this was one battle she wasn't going to win, but she would enjoy trying. She raised her head for Brett's kiss, revelling in its hard demand, giving herself entirely to the moment and all its heady pleasure, safe in the knowledge of his love.

'Stay with me,' she pleaded when he released her. 'I want to sleep in your arms.'

Now it was his turn to laugh.

'You already have. That night in Lerwick when we shared a bed. You were having a nightmare and it seemed a good way to stop you crying, although to tell the truth I was searching for an excuse anyway, and had been from the moment I kissed you. I went into that room, saw you, was determined to think the worst of you, probably because I knew I'd met my Waterloo, but the moment I held you in my arms I knew that there was no way I was ever going to let you out of my life. You were mine, although you've given me some bad moments. Will you mind being married to an oil-man?'

'A civil engineer,' Catriona corrected, a smile softening her lips. 'No. I think Magnus's accident threw me off balance. He told me himself I was being paranoic about the oil industry. Besides, how could I continue to hate it,' she said softly, 'when it brought me you? More than ample recompense for any harm it had done me.' A small smile curved her mouth. How silly she had been! Even as far back as that first night her body and heart had known what her mind had refused to admit; that she had found love in the arms of a stranger. But he was a stranger no longer, she reminded herself. She laughed, and Brett studied her.

'What's so funny?'

'I was just remembering—that first night in Lerwick. You said you weren't going to teach me how to make love.'

For a moment there was silence, and then desire smouldered darkly in his eyes.

'Just try and stop me,' he advised softly.

She met his kiss without restraint, gladly giving herself up to it—and him.